"What am I, a challenge or something?"

Diane spoke coldly. "A possible conquest for your male ego?"

Alex stiffened, and in the darkened room she heard him draw his breath. "No, I don't consider an emotional cripple a possible conquest. That is you, isn't it? You don't know how to feel."

"What's it to you?" she shouted suddenly. "I don't need your advice! I'm a perfectly normal healthy woman and I can take care of myself—"

"You can feed yourself, protect yourself, and never have to care for anybody else. What kind of existence is that? You never ache or cry or bleed for anybody else. You know, I pity you!"

Diana stood very still while his voice ripped her to shreds. Then she said one thing, devoid of all feeling or anger.

"Get out."

WELCOME
TO THE WONDERFUL WORLD
OF *Harlequin Romances*

Interesting, informative and entertaining,
each Harlequin Romance portrays an appealing
and original love story. With a varied array
of settings, we may lure you on an African safari,
to a quaint Welsh village, or an exotic Riviera
location—anywhere and everywhere that adventurous
men and women fall in love.

As publishers of Harlequin Romances, we're
extremely proud of our books. Since 1949,
Harlequin Enterprises has built its publishing
reputation on the solid base of quality and
originality. Our stories are the most popular
paperback romances sold in North America; every
month, six new titles are released and sold at
nearly every book-selling store in Canada and the
United States.

A free catalog listing all Harlequin Romances
can be yours by writing to the

HARLEQUIN READER SERVICE,
(In the U.S.) P.O. Box 52040, Phoenix, AZ 85072-2040
(In Canada) Stratford, Ontario, N5A 6W2

We sincerely hope you enjoy reading
this Harlequin Romance.

Yours truly,

THE PUBLISHERS
Harlequin Romances

A Deeper Dimension

Amanda Carpenter

Harlequin Books

TORONTO • NEW YORK • LONDON
AMSTERDAM • PARIS • SYDNEY • HAMBURG
STOCKHOLM • ATHENS • TOKYO • MILAN

Original hardcover edition published in 1983
by Mills & Boon Limited

ISBN 0-373-02605-6

Harlequin Romance first edition March 1984

CHAPTER ONE

LONG legs slid out and down and a gracefully slim body moved lithely after as the raven-haired young woman left her parked car. The construction worker watched her walk into the large, steel-constructed building, his face alight with interested amusement. He'd seen some tall girls in his day, and some good-looking girls too. But it was a fine, rare day when he saw a tall girl in which both qualities were combined to produce such a graceful beauty. As she moved through the glass doors to disappear into the building, he sighed with disappointment.

Diana had kept her face impassive throughout this perusal even while a bubble of laughter danced around in her stomach. The look on the man's face had been expressive, and she had always enjoyed men's reaction to her height and looks. She remembered a trip she had made to Italy, just after her senior year in college and before she started graduate school. It had been a cycling trip with a group of students, and Diana had towered a full head over the smaller Italians, creating a mild disturbance wherever she went.

Her swift pace now carried her quickly to the elevator and, after punching the button with the arrow pointing up, she allowed her gaze to travel calmly over the busy ground floor of Mason Steel. Several times people averted their eyes from hers or suddenly started animated conversations until her gaze slid past. One corner of her mouth quirked briefly. News travelled fast in a place like this, of that she was sure. That she was the current topic of discussion, she also had no doubt. By now everyone had heard of the—what would be the word?—new hot-shot from graduate school that Owen Bradshaw, the Personnel Manager, had hired for the administration department, to be personal assistant to the Big Man himself. That the executive assistant was to be a woman had probably heightened enthusiasm as the news flashed through the offices, for although more women than ever before now graduated with their Master's degree in Business Administration, their numbers were still relatively few and malicious opposition was considerable. The elevator doors slid open and the elevator operator gave a start as Diana, preoccupied with her thoughts, made a sound that was suspiciously like a snort. She looked down at him as she walked into the cubicle and grinned. The poor man looked uncertain as to whether he should grin back. 'Top floor, please,' she stated crisply, halfway regretting her smile.

The boy's features broke into a smile, however, and he gave a delighted exclamation. 'Hey! You that new hot-shot from grad school that everybody's talkin' about?'

She mentally rolled her eyes and congratulated herself on her excellent guess of words. 'Now,' she said aloud, 'how did you know that?'

He punched a button and the doors closed. ''Cause they ain't expectin' anyone else at the top,' he stated knowledgeably. Diana's eyebrows rose as he continued, 'Everybody round here calls Mr Mason's floor the "top", 'cause that's where all the hot-shots are—no offence.' His lively eyes danced at her.

While Diana tried to suppress her smile, she couldn't keep her eyes from dancing back at him, making him grin in appreciation. Her large eyes were a vivid golden honey heavily rimmed with long lashes and her eyebrows were arched on a high forehead. Her cheekbones were high and prominent and her nose long and thin. It was a strong face, yet with a refinement around the nostrils, and the curve of her mouth was undeniably feminine. Things, the young man thought to himself as he gazed around in satisfaction, were going to get interesting!

Diana was thinking the same thing, but her perusal was more grim. She fully realised that for the next few months she was going to be under surveillance. Every wrong move and mistake would be noted, and any indecision watched. A high-power organisation could not afford to have incompetents in charge and the ones who did not meet standards would be brushed aside, like so many flies, to make room for those who could.

Diana's quick brain and effortless grasp of difficult concepts had put her ahead early in school, and she had excelled in her graduate work in Business Administration, but now the real test had come. She had to sink or swim and she knew it. She looked back on all of the lean years behind her: all those years of barely squeezing by, desperately scraping enough money together to meet school fees, eating omelettes for dinner because she'd been too poor to buy anything else, hating to throw away a pair of old jeans because she would have to replace them somehow. She looked back, and that stubborn core of determination that hadn't let her stop and settle for something else, something easier, hardened one more time inside. She would damn well swim, or die trying!

The elevator stopped; the doors opened silently. Diana looked down the gleaming corridor and nodded. The struggle, she knew, was only beginning. She thanked the elevator boy and stepped out.

As she walked down the empty hallway, she was struck by the realisation that the emptiness was symbolic of her whole life. Every echoing step, sounding hollow in the silence, was like a tribute to the years of her childhood and her school life, her lack of family and her lack of true friends. Shuffled off from foster-home to foster-home, never knowing where she started or where she would end up, she was always alone and trying desperately hard not to show how lonely. This walk was fate's hand closing the gate to the past, the ending of a finished chapter in a book and the beginning of a new one.

She stood in front of the closed door that had 'Alexander Mason' printed in stark gold letters at eye level. She took a deep breath and told herself, 'I am capable and confident.' It helped just a little. She put out her hand, grasped the doorknob, and stepped in.

The office room that she stepped into was big and comfortable. To her right stood a large desk with a dark-haired woman behind it who appeared to be somewhere in her forties. To her left was a comfortable-looking couch, several plants, and two filing cabinets. A door was straight ahead. 'That way lies my destiny,' her irreverent sense of humour whispered dramatically. She told it firmly to shut up. The secretary behind the desk had looked up when Diana had come in, and she now came forward with a wide smile.

'You must be Diana Carrington!' the woman exclaimed as they shook hands. 'How do you do? I'm Alex Mason's secretary, Carrie Stevens.'

'Hello, Mrs Stevens,' replied Diana with a faint smile, noting the ring on the other woman's left hand.

'Oh dear, if you call me anything but Carrie, I'll be terribly hurt!' Brown eyes crinkled up in a smile as she looked up at Diana.

'Well,' she said, half laughing, 'in that case, you'd better call me Diana.'

'All right, Diana.' There was a warm friendliness about the older woman that Diana was instinctively drawn to. 'Alex is on the phone right now, but he'll be with you in just a few minutes. If you would like to have a seat over there on the couch, I'll be glad to get you some coffee.'

Diana smiled, this time quite warmly at the smaller woman. 'Thank you, that would be lovely.'

Carrie moved across the room, her actions quick and efficient. She spoke over her shoulder to Diana as she walked behind her desk to a very small table that was pushed up against the wall, with a coffee machine and cups on it. 'We like to keep a coffee maker here in the office, instead of running to the cafeteria every time we want a cup. It's so much more economical, a real time-saver. It's also very nice for when Alex has to work late hours.' Carrie handed her a Styrofoam cup of steaming coffee and Diana murmured her thanks.

'Please,' she begged, after taking the cup, 'don't let me keep you from your work.' She settled back and watched the other woman go back to her desk.

It was no good pretending that she wasn't nervous— she was, terribly so. Alexander Mason had been away on one of his many business trips when Owen Bradshaw had conducted the interviews for the job, so Diana had never even met him. She thought back on all she knew about him. Mason, age somewhere around thirty six, was an industrial and financial genius. He had somehow got hold of an iron ore company; Diana searched her mind for a name: Johnson's or Jackson's—Jackmon, that was it. Jackmon Steel had been foundering in the last throes of a dying business when Alexander Mason had bought it. In two years he had produced a profit from the company, although now it was Mason Steel. In the next three years, he had doubled the profits. Now, nine years later, he had an administration building in New York, steel foundries in Pittsburgh and Philadelphia, and offices in San Francisco. The growth of the business was nothing less than phenomenal. Alexander Mason's private life was something she could only guess at. Frequently his name appeared in both the financial section and the gossip section in New York newspapers. The man not only worked hard but he played hard too. The papers labelled him as a bit of a playboy and frequently linked his name with those of the female sex. At any rate, Diana had no desire to find out for herself whether he was a playboy or not. She simply didn't care.

As she had been busy mulling over the intriguing gossip that she had read about Alexander Mason, she was vaguely aware of a buzzer sounding and a murmur of voices. She looked up as Carrie spoke to her. 'Alex has completed his call, Diana,' she said in her pleasant voice. 'He asked me to let you know that you can go in now,' and she indicated the door to Diana's left.

'Thank you,' said Diana, wishing she could think of something else to say to her. She deposited her cup in the small waste basket by Carrie's desk and moved to the door. She schooled her thoughts into severely disciplined channels and smoothed away any expression on her face. Putting her hand on the door handle, she was startled to have it wrenched out of her grip as the door swept open. She was even more startled to find herself looking into the most vivid pair of blue eyes that she had ever seen—and she was looking up! The moment stretched on and she picked up other impressions of chestnut brown hair, an angularly handsome face, and a strongly shaped mouth that was beginning to twitch. Her eyes flew to his, but she could see no hint of humour there. She decided she must be imagining it.

The door opened wider and the tall man spoke, 'Diana Carrington? Please come in.' He turned and walked away from the door, leaving her to shut it behind her. Diana watched quietly as he prowled about the office. Her first impression was right about his height; he was a big man, well over six foot, with a broad chest and shoulders that narrowed into trim hips and thighs and long, muscular legs. One of her eyebrows rose ever so faintly as she realised that her perusal was being returned. Other than that, her face had no expression, and she patiently stood waiting. He positioned himself against the front of the desk in a leaning posture and gestured to the chair in front of him. Diana, flicking a glance around her, walked over to the seat and sat down. She crossed her legs deliberately and unhurriedly, made sure she was comfortable, then looked up, surprising a strange look on his face.

He spoke, 'By now, I'm sure you've realised that I'm Alex Mason.' It was said in a dry voice, tinged with sarcasm. Diana took it to be an introduction and, ignoring the sarcasm, nodded. He went on, 'Owen Bradshaw, whom you've met and talked to, gave me his notes on your interview and your résumé.' He reached behind him and picked up some papers, then continued, 'Diana Carrington, age twenty-six, graduate of Rhydon University in Business Administration—what do you know about steel?' The question was swift and unexpected.

Diana said carefully, 'I know a great deal less than you do, Mr Mason.'

His eyebrows shot down and he growled, 'What the hell is that supposed to mean?'

Her eyebrows had shot up at his tone and words. She explained, 'I know that you saved a company by difficult strategic manoeuvring, and that you doubled profits in three years, and your company is growing by leaps and bounds. This I can understand, analyse, and even chart for you if you wish. I can tell you when you decided to do what you did and why. The business side of this company I can understand—it's what I studied for years. Steel, as I told Mr Bradshaw, is as foreign a subject to me as what makes a car run.' This last was said with a touch of self-directed mockery.

His mouth twitched, this time she was sure. He chuckled and commented dryly, 'At least that old dog hired someone with a sense of humour.' His face became serious and he continued, speaking concisely, 'Steel is an alloy, a mixture, if you like, of several different materials, including iron ore, coal and limestone. Measurement has to be exact, as exact as one thousandth of an ounce. By the time you're fully trained . . .' at his choice of words, Diana felt a little like a dog sent to training school. '. . . you'll know the prices and quantities of the raw materials we need, the most dependable suppliers, the costs of labour and equipment annually, and you'll be able to project profit estimates for the year ahead. I want you to start these proposals here and tell me your opinion for a counter-proposal for a contract to Nelson Ore . . .'

Diana accepted the paper folders that he gave her, and for the rest of the morning they argued and deliberated over the various approaches for the contract to their main supplier of iron ore. After that, without a rest, he took her over the entire building, ordered a desk for her use to be moved upstairs in his office, held an emergency conference with Owen Bradshaw about temporary labour to be hired owing to a bout of 'flu going around in one of the factories, and called California to clear up a problem in the San Francisco office. Her mind was whirling by the time they stopped for some quick sandwiches and a cup of coffee. They ate up in his office to save time.

Watching him in between bites of her sandwich, Diana marvelled at his incredible energy. The man fairly sent sparks of electricity into the air, she thought to herself.

'. . . sandwich?'

She started.

Alex (for that was what she called him in her mind) repeated patiently, 'Do you want another sandwich?'

'Thanks, yes.' She took it gratefully, and was unprepared for his chuckle. 'What did I do?' she asked, frowning slightly.

'Still a growing girl, aren't you, my dear?' Alex had a faint smile as he took in her tall frame. 'You're damn near as tall as I am.'

Diana, determined to take his ribbing in her stride, was angry at herself for colouring faintly at the way he was looking at her. She saw his grin widen and realised that he knew what she was thinking. She swallowed a mouthful of sandwich and laconically pronounced, 'Six feet in my stockings, sir.' She took another bite of sandwich.

He pretended to look surprised. 'Six feet tall!' he exclaimed with a note of wonder. Then, swiftly, 'And don't ever call me "sir" again in that tone of voice, my girl, or I'll turn you over my knee—yes, all six feet of you, and whack you over the bottom. I'm a bit bigger than you still.'

She was taken aback. 'What in the world!' she gasped. 'What was the tone of voice that I used, Mr Mason?'

Mr Mason leaned back in his chair. 'You quite deliberately tried to put me in my place for teasing you, and you know it.' He surveyed her lazily and continued, 'I was never one for learning my place.'

Diana had put that tone of standoffishness in her voice when she spoke, but it had been from force of habit, a habit she had acquired a long time ago when she had never been quite sure if the teaser had meant to be cruel or not. It had become an unconscious mannerism over the years, and people, once rebuffed, tended to stay away. Now she took a safe retreat by commenting, 'The sandwiches are very good.'

Alex smiled slowly, a gleam in his eyes, and Diana hurriedly offered him another sandwich. His third, she noted. He deliberately waited a moment to let her know that he realised a red herring when he saw it and then took the sandwich with a dry thanks.

A quick look at the clock on the desk had them gulping their food and coffee down in order to be on time for an afternoon conference with several of the different department heads. The afternoon flew by incredibly fast for Diana in an exhilarating way. Alexander Mason was simply fascinating to her—he stimulated her thinking and emotions like no other person that she knew. In that one afternoon, she saw several sides to his personality. One moment he was clicking ideas off of the top of his head like a computer, the next minute he would roar with fury or laughter. He was—intense, Diana thought as they hurried back to the top floor. The word, one that she had been groping for in a vague way, left her feeling uncomfortable. She did not like intensity; she shied away from it like a colt shying away from an unexpected noise. It frightened and confused her. In no way had she ever been exposed to any intense emotions. The past relationships she had experienced were generally those of a passive nature, a mutual reaction of sterile politeness, with no fights and no arguments, and also no loving or caring. She was, with Alex, very much at a loss.

She and Alex reached the office and both sank into chairs. Much to her own surprise, Diana felt wet with sweat. They had worked with so much intensity and singlemindedness that she hadn't had time to notice how physically drained she was. They sat in silence for a few moments. Then, with a suddeness that made her jump, he said, 'You have a smudge on your nose.'

'Thanks,' she said wryly, and rubbed the offending member. She started to chuckle and shake her head. He began to smile.

'Now, what did I say that was so funny?' he asked, his strong teeth showing white against a light tan. It seemed to hit her somewhere in the region of her stomach. Slightly disorientated, she looked at him and blinked.

'Oh—' she started, somewhat at a loss. Then she started to chuckle again. 'Someone else would have pointed out the mistakes that I made today, or tell me how well I did, or even just tell me to go home. But you? Oh, you tell me I have a smudge on my nose!'

Alex leaned back in his chair, his hands clasped behind his neck. 'And would you like to hear how well you did today?' he asked. One of his eyebrows was cocked in a way that she wasn't sure she liked. She considered the question seriously. Finally, with a rueful shake of the head, she smiled.

'No, I wouldn't. I would like to hear that I did well, and I'm not sure I did. I was too ignorant to have been of any real use to you today,' she said honestly.

Alex's face turned serious also, and he answered her quietly, 'Yes, you were, but you also had some very bright ideas today, for all your ignorance and inexperience. I was pleased with you and your work today. You did well.'

Diana glowed. This man's opinion was something that she found she respected, and his compliment made her happier than she would have liked to admit. Her face was carefully expressionless, but her eyes had a bit of a shine that they hadn't had before, and Alex's eyes were keener than she knew. He was suddenly brisk.

'I would like you to take these papers home to study. They contain information concerning our past contracts and per-cent output. Also, towards the back, I have some proposals that I'd like you to prepare an opinion on for tomorrow. Can you manage to be here around eight in the morning?' She nodded, secretly shocked. He continued, 'Good. We have a lot to do tomorrow before eleven. Plan on having lunch like we did today, there's not going to be much time between meetings. By tomorrow your desk should be here and we'll see about getting you settled in.'

'Shall I type up a summary and appraisal of these proposals?' she asked, frowning in concentration as she leafed through the pages he handed her.

'It would be a good idea.'

'All right. Anything else you would like?' Diana suddenly saw things in the question as soon as she said it, and she wished she had phrased it differently. Alex, however, answered her seriously. 'No, I think you have quite enough to do with just what I've given you.' He glanced at his watch. 'And for right now, I think you'd better get home so you can get to work.'

She chuckled, 'Whatever you say, boss.'

Swiftly glancing at her, he retorted, 'That's right, my girl. Whatever I say.'

'And what you say goes. Isn't that what you mean?' she teased, and getting up, she moved to the door. She had the most uncomfortable feeling of being watched, but refused to look around.

Alex said lazily, 'Hey, lady,' and she turned. He stated clearly, 'I'll remind you about that remark some day. Just so that you know whose say goes first.'

Diana sketched a smart salute and went out while listening to Alex's laughter.

Making her way through the outer office, she noticed that Carrie had already gone home, then stopped in shocked surprise. Already? Checking her wristwatch, she saw it was nearing six-thirty. Hurrying out the door and to the elevator, she marvelled at the way the day had flown by. Making her way out of the building and to the space where her car was parked, she glanced towards the construction site several yards away, but it was empty. She unlocked her car and got in.

New York traffic was, as usual, hectic and maddening. Finally reaching the outskirts of the downtown section,

Diana managed to make a little better time in the suburban areas. Her mind, however, was not occupied with the time it took to get to her little apartment, located in a converted old house in a relatively quiet part of the country. It was well out of the confines of the city, close to Elmsford, and Diana much preferred to commute to work so that she could enjoy more peaceful surroundings. Right now, she happened to be busy contemplating the motives and desires of the remarkable man she worked for. Somehow, after meeting and working with Alexander Mason, she could not reconcile her preconceived notions of him with her real-life impressions. She had thought of him before as the sort of man that would do anything for profit or gain and not be bothered by his conscience. That he was a shrewd businessman was certain, but the ruthless tycoon that the newspapers criticised was not the impression that she had got. Of course, she wisely realised that she had yet to see all the different sides to the man's personality, but what she had seen so far, she had liked. Liked maybe too much. Shaking her head as she turned down the side street that led to her apartment, she resolved not to think about it.

That, however, was hard to do. Letting herself into the apartment, she paused to kick off her shoes with a sigh, before going into her small kitchen to whip herself up a quick supper. She found herself moving in quick, hurried movements around the kitchen as if she were to dash back to work like they had for lunch. Sighing wryly, she admitted to herself how much she was still keyed up. She decided to get out her homework for the night and get that out of the way while she was still in the mood.

Looking at the different notes that Alex had given her, she again found herself thinking in high gear and coming up with ideas quicker than she could get them on to paper. Finding a major flaw in one of the contract proposals, she sat down at her typewriter to try and figure out a revision. The typewriter keys fairly flew as her fingers moved in pace with her thoughts.

Three hours later, she leaned back in her chair with a tired sigh. It had taken more time and work than she had anticipated, but she had finally come up with a type of contract proposal that would be close to acceptable, providing Alex liked it. Her mouth twisted and she corrected herself, 'Providing Mr Mason liked it.'

Now she was so tired that she barely took time to perform the actions necessary for going to bed before stumbling over to crawl between the covers. She caught herself before she drifted too close to sleep and remembered to set her alarm for five o'clock in the morning. After fiddling with the alarm, she rolled over and was almost asleep before she was settled.

Darkness and loud noise: A loud steady, buzzing noise that sounded very close, very like . . . her alarm! Diana rolled over and, trying to see her clock, made a grab for the general direction and missed. Grabbing again, she succeeded in locating the clock, but instead of getting hold of it, she only managed to push it farther away from her and out of reach. By now she was fully awake and fully annoyed with the raucous noise emanating from that damn clock. She bounced out of bed, turned on the bedroom light and switched off the alarm. Then she went over to the window, a big, cheerful affair that was intended to let a lot of fresh sunlight and air in. She felt like swearing. The sun wasn't even up at five o'clock! She grumbled, 'God knows any sane person wouldn't be,' and went to make herself some coffee. While it was brewing, she padded off to her bedroom again to sort out an outfit to wear, then she went off to start some hot bath water. After a good reviving soak in the tub and steamy cup of coffee, she felt almost human again.

Sitting in her bedroom in front of her dresser mirror, she took stock of her appearance. Shadows were under her eyes from such a short night's sleep and her face looked to herself to be a pasty sort of pudding colour. Resignedly, she reached for her make-up jars. Fifteen minutes later, a vibrant, glowing face looked back when she peered in the mirror. 'Thank the Lord for such wonderful blessings as coffee-makers and cosmetics!' she looked towards heaven as she muttered.

Another fifteen minutes and she was on her way.

Knots of tension slowly hardened in her stomach as she tried to cope with the thickening traffic and her own shortening temper. Her nerves were stretched very thinly during the next forty minutes or so that it took her to commute to the New York office. Her confidence dwindled with the passing miles as she thought of what she *could* have done with the revised proposal. She felt even worse when she considered that she hadn't even started on the other proposals that Alex had given her.

Diana, reaching the parking lot reserved for the workers at Mason Steel, ended up parking not with a sigh of relief from the journey's end but with a groan of apprehension at the day ahead. Moving towards the building, she mentally composed herself for the immediate future.

The stares were again directed her way as she walked to the elevator doors, but this time she did not really notice. All her attention was concentrated on her own thoughts. She walked on into the cubicle.

'Say there! Hi, Miss Carrington, remember me?' asked the young elevator operator. She blinked a little in surprise at having her reverie interrupted, then she smiled.

'Of course I remember you,' she said warmly, looking down at him with friendliness. The young man had the same engaging grin. 'You never told me your name, though.'

He looked pleased. 'No, ma'am, I didn't. My first name is Jerry. I'd be honoured if you called me that, ma'am.'

Diana laughed. 'All right, Jerry it is.'

Jerry looked at her a little hesitantly. 'How do you like working for Mr Mason, Miss Carrington?' he asked. His tone of voice had a note of awe in it. Diana was privately amused. However, she knew better than to show it.

She answered quietly, 'I don't really know how I'll feel once I'm settled in, but right at the moment I'm quite enjoying it. Mr Mason is very nice.'

Jerry's eyes lit up, and he asked enthusiastically, 'Do you really think so, too? I think he's the most kindest man in the whole world!'

Wondering what 'Mr Mason' had done to deserve such fervent praise, she commented, 'I wonder if he evokes that kind of response from all his employees.'

'Oh, I don't know, ma'am! But if he does half as much for the rest of them as he does for me . . .' and there he stopped with a hand clapped over his mouth in a most tantalising way. Diana had looked at Jerry with an increasing interest as he had talked, and was very intrigued with the secretive way he had left the statement open. She just couldn't resist.

'What does he do for you, Jerry?'

He looked at her doubtfully. 'He made me promise not to tell anyone.' He chewed his lower lip in an agony of indecision. She opened her mouth to speak when he said suddenly, 'I bet he tells you all sorts of secrets and you never tell a soul. Well, I'll tell you.'

Diana protested, 'Jerry, I don't think you should.'

He grinned. 'But I want someone to know how nice Mr Mason is, and all. You see, I quit high school when I was sixteen, 'cause I didn't think I needed it. But Mr Mason talked me into goin' back to school and finishin' my education. Well, I said, 'Mr Mason, I just can't afford to do that, 'cause I'm just barely squeezin' by as it is.' Mr Mason just looked at me and he says, 'Don't you worry about it, son. Just you go and enrol for some night courses and I'll take care of the rest.'

'So I went on down to the school nearest my neighbourhood, and enrolled the very next day. And do you know what happened when I got my next pay-check, Miss Carrington? I got a two and a half dollar raise! Two and a half dollars! 'Course, I got to work my hours to get the money, but Miss Carrington, that was the nicest thing anybody has ever done for me in my life. I can even afford to buy new clothes if I need them!' Diana felt a peculiar lump as she heard these words.

She said sincerely, 'Jerry, I think it's the nicest thing I've ever heard of anybody doing for someone else, giving a person the chance to better his own life by education.'

He said solemnly, 'Yes, ma'am, and I'm goin' to repay his kindness some day. Just you wait and see, some day I'm goin' to do somethin' for him.'

Diana noticed that the elevator had stopped and the doors had been open for some time. 'Oh, lord, if I don't get to work, I don't think Mr Mason is going to be nice to me at all,' she laughed, and shook her head at Jerry.

He smiled too, then said earnestly, 'If I might say so, Miss Carrington, it is nice to have you here.'

Looking down that empty corridor once again, she turned her head and answered quietly, 'Thank you, Jerry. I think I'll find it nice to be here. I'll see you later.' She stepped out into the hall.

'Have a nice day, Miss Carrington,' he called before the doors closed shut.

Diana grimaced, remembering the unread reports in her arms. The day hadn't even begun, and she wasn't very sure that it would be at all nice.

She walked into Carrie's office and glanced at the desk.

It was empty. She probably didn't get here until nine o'clock or so, Diana surmised. Moving to the other door, she knocked lightly and waited.

'Come in!' a voice snapped. It had a particularly ominous tone, a foreboding of bad temper and little patience.

She opened the door and stepped lightly in, and was immediately struck anew by the physical largeness of the man as she quietly moved into the room. Now that she was actually looking at him, she couldn't believe that she would ever get used to his bulk. Alex was pacing the room in long angry strides, his hair ruffled up as if he had been raking his fingers through it. He wore a dark grey pair of slacks and a grey waistcoat over a white shirt, and his tie was loosened. A jacket lay across the back of his chair in a crumpled-up fashion, and Diana inwardly winced to think of such a lovely expensive material being so abused. She automatically went to straighten it up, and was halted by the harshness of Alex's voice.

He snapped, 'Where the hell have you been?'

She turned in amazement. 'Am I late?' she asked in surprise. She looked at the small desk clock. It read three minutes past eight o'clock. She had walked in to the office one minute late. She turned towards Alex, frowning a little in puzzlement. 'I'm not all that late, surely? You did say eight, didn't you?'

Sighing in exasperation, Alex nodded and ran his fingers through his hair, ruffling it up even worse. He stood with one hand on his hip and acknowledged, 'Yes, I did say eight. I'm sorry I snapped at you like that.' It was said briefly, absentmindedly. Almost, she thought with resentment, as if he didn't really mean it. Alex had continued talking. '. . . gave you a report last night that I needed to have read by morning, do you remember going over the Anderson report last night?'

Diana, feeling a little uncomfortable, said quietly, 'That was on the bottom of the pile, I'm afraid, and I didn't get to them all.'

Alex's head snapped around and his eyes narrowed. 'You didn't get to them all,' he repeated in a very quiet voice. 'Pray tell, what did you get to?'

She put the different folders down and searched through them. 'Here,' she said, 'I studied the Nelson proposal. There were a lot of problems I found in it, but the main problem was the wording used in the agreements. What they basically did was use a lot of words that really promised nothing. I sat down last night and retyped the whole thing. It took me several hours and I didn't get to anything else.'

Alex walked over to the desk and, barely looking at the proffered revision, snapped, 'That's just great! The one report that could have waited a few days, and that had to be the only one you did! Where did you put the Anderson report?' He started to rummage around in the pile.

Diana felt a slow burning anger starting to flare up somewhere around her midriff, but said calmly enough, 'Maybe I can help you with it to make things go faster.'

He didn't look up. 'No,' he said shortly, 'I don't want help,' sounding, to her, like a child refusing help to tie his shoelaces.

She said, unable to stop herself, 'Maybe I should go out and come back in to see if we can start off on a better foot!'

This time he did look up. His eyes were narrowed and he looked every bit as angry as she felt. 'That,' he said very evenly, 'won't be necessary. Just finish the reports and proposals that you didn't do last night.'

Diana flushed. 'I'm sorry about not getting to all of them,' she offered quietly.

'So am I.' He didn't look at her, and his tone was short.

'Look,' she began, feeling goaded by his lack of under-standing, 'are you going to want to beat me for it? I did my best.'

'Let's just forget it, all right?' he snapped, his blue eyes and rigid jawline showing frustration. He half-turned away from her and began to scan the papers held in his hand as he continued, 'Your best just didn't happen to be what I needed.'

Diana began to whistle soundlessly through her teeth. 'Why do I feel like excess baggage?' she remarked to the room in general.

'What do you want me to do—pat you on the back for something you failed to do?' Alex threw down the papers and swivelled back to face her, his face ominous.

'Hey, I didn't fail at anything,' she responded swiftly, stabbing the air in front of her with one hand. 'There was just too much material for one evening.'

'If you can't handle the work load . . .' he began nastily. Enough was enough, Diana decided abruptly. If she didn't get out right away, she would say something she would regret.

'Get out of the kitchen if you can't stand the heat, is that it?' she asked stiffly. Without another word she pivoted on her heel and headed for the door. She heard a groan behind her.

'Diana!' Alex called. She kept on going, partly for fear of what she might say to him if she stayed, partly from fear of what he might say to her. Every step got faster and faster and her temper got closer and closer to the edge of control. By the time she had reached the door, she was walking very fast, and she wrenched it open stormed through and slammed the door shut behind her. Eyes glowing with fury, she barely took in the fact that Carrie was standing behind her desk in the act of taking off a sweater. She swept by, ignoring Carrie's greeting, and threw open the outer door. By this time Alex had the first door open and he called again, 'Diana! Come back a moment—damn it, girl, I said come back!'

CHAPTER TWO

DIANA was out into the corridor and going swiftly down the hall before he caught up with her. She felt something grab hold of her arm and suddenly she was jerked around to face a very big man.

She hissed at him, 'Will you let go of my arm, please, before I say something to you that I shouldn't!' He was silent, and she stared up into his face with a puzzled anger.

He seemed infuriatingly calm as his eyes went over her face. Diana was breathing rather heavily from her temper and her colour was higher than usual. Eyes emanating sparks glared back at him. She looked very beautiful.

He turned back to the office and started walking back, never letting go of her arm. Diana immediately began to pull back and resist.

He growled, 'Not now, all right?' and kept going.

Back at the outer office, Carrie sat behind her desk with her mouth slightly open as they stomped back through to the inner room. Neither one paid any attention, though, and the door slammed one more time as Alex and Diana disappeared.

He let go of her arm when they reached the privacy of his office and moved to the front of the desk to lean against it, rubbing his eyes. 'I'm a bad-tempered son of a bitch.' This brought Diana's eyes to him quickly, and she looked at him more closely. She saw lines radiating from tired-looking eyes, lines she hadn't noticed before, and a faint stubble of beard. She suddenly thought to herself, 'Good lord, it doesn't look as if he got any sleep last night!'

She said abruptly and aloud, 'How much sleep did you get last night? Any at all?'

He peered at her from over the hand covering his face and said flatly, 'None.'

'What happened?' Diana responded immediately. He didn't reply for a moment.

Then he said, 'The workers at the Pittsburgh factory went on strike last night unexpectedly. They'd been threatening it for a few weeks, but Dobson, the factory foreman, had told me they were settling down. That contract for Steve Anderson was to have been shipped by the end of the week. Now I'm not sure we can even get enough steel poured by the end of this week, let alone put on freight cars and shipped to Anderson's factories.'

Diana, in a swift, comprehending flash, took in all the unsaid implications. There was a great deal of money that the company could lose, besides the irrevocable blemish of a contract unfulfilled. She let out her breath in a long sigh as she stared at nothing. Alex's voice brought her eyes to focus on him.

He asked quietly, 'If I tell you I'm sorry for yelling at you like I did, and say what a rotten-tempered pig I am, will you forgive me for being so rude?'

She considered him with her head cocked to one side. Her eyes crinkled in a smile as she replied humorously, 'Yes—only if you say you're a rotten pig!'

One side of his mouth tugged upwards. 'Consider it done.'

Diana had never worked so furiously in all her life as she worked that day. Alex was planning to take an early evening flight to Pittsburgh, which made the day even shorter for them. She had panicked when he had told her that he was to be gone for a few days, and that he would relay instructions to her from there. She had a horrible feeling of inadequacy, a feeling that any decision she made would end up being wrong, terribly wrong.

She said as much to Alex as they drove the company car to the airport. 'I feel very unsure of myself,' she confessed to him, watching his hands on the steering wheel. They looked strong and capable as he handled the car patiently in the midst of traffic. 'I know virtually nothing about what to do if a crisis comes up.'

Alex flicked her a glance, and she caught the flash of blue eyes. 'All you need to do is to relay instructions that I give you. Nothing should come up in the next two days that's out of the ordinary. If you have a problem deciding what needs to be done, ask either Owen Bradshaw, Carrie, or call my number in Pittsburgh. I don't expect any major problems, or else I wouldn't be going. Besides, Diana, I respect your judgment.'

Diana looked out the window and wished she felt as confident as Alex. 'Thank you, Mr Mason,' she said quietly. 'I hope I can live up to that respect.'

Half laughing with exasperation, he asked her, 'Everyone else in the office is on a first-name basis, Diana. I've even noticed you called Carrie by her first name today. Do you think you could bring yourself to call me by my first name? And please make it "Alex" and not "Alexander"!'

Diana smiled and asked, 'What happens to people who call you Alexander?'

He started to grin. 'Well,' he drawled in a deliberating tone, 'I used to beat up anyone at school who tried to tease me by calling me Alexander. I suppose now I'd turn anyone smaller than me over my knee, since it's almost as bad as calling me "sir".' Stopped at a redlight, he turned his head, and Diana could see the proud lines of his posture. 'Are you thinking about trying out my full name to see if you can get away with it?'

She ignored the challenging tone in his voice and

ejected a note of shock in her own. 'Good heavens, no!' she exclaimed haughtily. 'I wouldn't dream of calling you anything but Alex, Mr Mason.'

The light turned green, and Alex looked at her for a long moment with a smile before he pulled out.

At the airport, he pulled into a space at the kerb that was used for loading and unloading passengers, and turned the car engine off. He said quickly, 'I'd appreciate it if you drove this car while I'm gone, and do you think you could pick me up when I get back?'

She replied, 'Of course.'

'Good. And Diana?' She looked at him with a questioning lift of her eyebrows. Alex smiled crookedly and said, 'You did well on the Nelson proposal. I looked at it when I went home to pack. Use it tomorrow at the business meeting.' At her startled protest, he raised a hand imperiously. 'I've already told Owen that I wanted him there, so if you have any problems, rely on his help. All right?' He was looking at her hard.

Diana's mouth was open to protest and she closed it with a resigned nod.

'That's my girl,' he affirmed. He opened up the car door and got out, and she watched his long body unfold itself. Waiting until she had slid over to sit in the driver's seat, he reached in the back to pick up his suitcase. Then he turned back to her and leaned in through the open window. 'Wish me luck,' he said to her.

Staring into those blue, blue eyes so close to her, she laughed a rather unsteady laugh.

'Wish me luck, you mean,' she replied wryly. Alex smiled, a deep steady glow in his eyes.

'To both of us, then,' he offered, and as she nodded, he kissed her swiftly on the side of the mouth. 'I'll call you,' he promised, and strode swiftly away.

Diana sat for some time in the car, staring straight

ahead at nothing. Alex's mouth had felt warm and firm on her cheek and it had evoked a strange response within her. Just for a moment she had felt like laughing, like crying, like putting her arms around him and kissing him back . . . she jerked her thoughts away from that direction. Emotions, she told herself as calmly as possible, were transitory. Physical responses have nothing to do with the intellect. She put the car into drive and started away, still trying to convince herself that she believed what she was saying. On her way back to the office, she was struck with an icy cold wave of hard thought. 'Snap out of it, my girl,' she spoke out loud to emphasise her own words. They echoed too loudly in the confines of the car. 'You're not being rational. You were in a vicious argument with him less than five hours ago. You didn't know him the day before yesterday. What are you thinking?'

At the office, she spent the rest of the afternoon preparing for the business meeting the next morning. She tried to tell herself that there was nothing to be nervous about, but her stomach called herself a liar. It was all twisted in knots, growling and grumbling like a bad-tempered bear.

Stacking the papers once more to make sure she had everything, she looked at her watch. Six o'clock. She looked around the office to see if there was anything she could put in order before she left. The room, big and comfortable, was panelled in a muted dark brown with a light beige carpeting and two armchairs facing Alex's desk. Her smaller desk was positioned on the other side of the room with a filing cabinet pushed up against the wall behind. A large picture window facing the door leading to the outer office let in a great deal of light and added a touch of spaciousness to the room. Diana privately thought the room was bare and empty without the man for whom it was designed. Closing the curtains, she turned and left, a little depressed. Carrie was gone again; late hours seemed to be the normal state of things for Diana around here.

She drove the company car carefully home and parked it beside the house where she lived. She noticed that Terry and Brenda, the people who rented the ground floor of the house, were gone, and she remembered them saying something about going to visit Brenda's grandparents for a few days. It gave her a lonely feeling to know that she was the only one in the house, for it was big and made strange noises late at night. She ate a light supper and got ready for an early night, telling herself that she didn't really expect Alex to call tonight anyway and that the creaking of the big house was what made her feel all alone. She slept badly.

The alarm clock and the phone went off simultaneously. At first, Diana was at a loss, for she couldn't distinguish between the two noises. Then, with a bound, she was out of bed, switching off the alarm, and lurching to grab the phone before its sixth ring.

'Hello,' she mumbled tiredly into the receiver, rubbing her eyes and trying not to yawn. The voice on the other end was irritatingly fresh and crisp.

'Hello, sleepyhead,' Alex's disembodied voice sounded startlingly close and clear.

'If you call at—what is it?—good lord, five o'clock in the morning, you can't expect a whole lot else,' Diana, giving in, yawned as she spoke. 'I didn't really expect you to call until tonight to see how the business meeting went.'

'I didn't really need to call until tonight. I just called to give you a boost of self-confidence. You'll do fine today, Diana.'

She felt suddenly reassured at the tone in Alex's voice as he spoke. It was just the right mixture of briskness, businesslike and calm, yet with a note of warmth that made the loneliness of the night a shadowy thing of the past, half forgotten in the events of the day. She sighed. 'Oh, do you think so? I've been almost sick with worry.'

A thread of amusement was in his voice, this time as he answered, 'I thought that would probably be the case. Dear Diana, so anxious to do well and so worried that you won't. How you made it through life without my reassurance, I don't know. Life must have been tough.'

Diana stirred a little as she took in his words. She knew Alex was merely teasing her in a light way to ease her own tension, but he inadvertently only managed to evoke memories that were better left buried. He had hit too close to home. She had always lived with a slight uneasiness that maybe, if she wasn't careful, she would mess up, make a fool of herself, and this fear of failure had always goaded her into perfectionism. As she thought of this, she remembered yesterday's argument with Alex, and her own response, her lack of control. She also remembered how she had reacted to his lighthearted kiss of farewell at the airport, and suddenly realised why she couldn't seem to keep her cool around him. He saw too much. He saw beyond the illusion of her thick wall, and got under her skin. Distance must be put between them.

All this flashed through her head in a split second. She asked quickly, 'How are things going there?'

There was a brief pause, then Alex said starkly, 'Bad. I've been meeting some of the labour spokesmen and they seem to be riled about something rumoured to have been cut from the Philadelphia factory's pay benefits. They think it's going to happen to them next. I haven't figured out just exactly what's going on here, but what I've heard doesn't make sense. There's something wrong and that something smells like the proverbial kettle of fish. Why would a rumour like that get started when it has no basis? And if it has no basis, why are the men upset?'

Diana wrinkled her brow, 'It just doesn't make any sense! It's illogical.'

He replied, and there was a hard note that she hadn't yet heard in his voice, a note of steel. 'What I'm afraid of is that it's all too logical and I'm not going to like whatever it is. Something is wrong, and I intend to find out what it is, and when I do, there's going to be hell to pay!'

Diana felt a little of Alex's baffled anger at the apparently senseless actions of the men who, just recently, had had the best record in that state for behaviour and performance.

They talked a few minutes more before Alex told her he was due back for another conference in five minutes. 'I'll call again tonight to see how your meeting went,' he concluded. 'Good luck, and be good today, Diana.'

'Alex?' she spoke seriously. 'Try to rest when you can, all right? Working two nights through is no good for the body, and the brain is only flesh too. Rest up, okay?'

'Will do, ma'am. Owen told me you seemed to have a firm hand. Do you flog people too?' Alex chuckled as he spoke.

Diana ordered exasperatedly, 'Just say goodbye and go, will you?'

'I'll talk to you later. Diana?'

'Yes.'

'Thanks.'

She met Owen Bradshaw in Alex's office before they went down to the conference room on the third floor. They were to meet the Nelson representatives at eleven o'clock to reach an agreement over the two conflicting contract proposals. She was glad Owen was to be there, for he was a tower of strength and an invaluable source of information. Diana watched him as he talked with her, her mind vaguely registering the incongruity of the man.

Owen Bradshaw was indeed an interesting and complex man, surprisingly so, for the one impression that people invariably received was one of simplicity. He had very neat hands and feet, and a plumpish body that bounced as he walked. His face was an unassuming and unspectacular sort that wore a perpetual and sunny expression of vagueness as if the mind behind it had no intelligence whatsoever. Owen Bradshaw had the keenest and quickest mind in the business with the exception of Alex Mason. He had a particular talent for being able to rattle off ideas, facts, and theories faster than his listeners could follow, and all the while wearing the same benign, idiotic expression.

He was talking to her now as they headed to the elevator. 'The fellows from the Nelson manufacturers are a bigger nuisance than their orders are worth,' Owen sighed with exasperation. 'They're like scared rabbits who jump at the slightest noise of unrest in the economy. Chances are that since Alex isn't here, they're going to be hellish to handle.'

They stepped into the elevator, still talking. After nodding a greeting to Jerry, Diana asked Owen, 'Are they likely to be upset with having to deal with a woman?'

He hesitated. 'Probably,' he admitted after a moment. 'It's unavoidable, of course, because we wouldn't dream of discriminating on the basis of sex, and we stand behind all our employees. You, Diana, are the one who should conduct this meeting, and if others can't handle it, they can take their business somewhere else. Real professionals deal with charts and facts, not skirts or pants.'

'But what if I lose the contract?' she protested. They were heading towards the conference doors now. Owen paused with his hand on the knob.

'Most people are too smart to cut their own throats by refusing to deal with us. We're the best suppliers of steel in this part of the nation. They may resent you, but they won't do anything too foolish,' he whispered. Then he opened the door and politely allowed Diana to precede him.

He then turned to the group of men already at the table who had risen at their entrance. 'Gentlemen, I'd like to introduce you to Mr Mason's executive assistant, Miss Diana Carrington.' Owen gave Diana a warm smile as he spoke. 'We're very proud of her.'

Diana allowed none of the warmth that she felt as she heard these words to show. She surveyed the five men who were being introduced to her. There was an unconsciously regal incline to the tilt of her head that hadn't been there before, and her eyes calmly met those of each of the men, showing no hint of intimidation or trepidation. Her voice was brisk as she greeted them all, allowing and receiving no nonsense.

The meeting as it progressed was baffling and infuriating. The men had apparently accepted her with no problems, yet they all acted with a caginess when presented with Mason's counter-proposal that was completely illogical. Diana's proposal had been concise to the point of terseness to avoid any loopholes in the agreements. It was fair and reasonable, and yet the other men disagreed with every phrase. When asked what they disagreed with, they vaguely murmured something about the wording being unacceptable. When asked for a better alternative, they simply shrugged their shoulders.

Diana put up with this farce of a business meeting for the better part of an hour. Then she suddenly put down the papers she'd been holding and started stacking everything together. 'Gentlemen, I believe the meeting is over with,' she stated, a thread of controlled anger in her voice. 'You apparently don't want a reasonable proposal, and you can't come in with an alternative of your own. Please call us and cancel the meeting the next time you wish to be so unreasonable. Our time is too valuable to be wasted like this.'

Owen had got up at her words and, as she turned to walk out of the room, he was right behind her and quickly closing the doors after them. She continued to walk rapidly down the hall and Owen had to trot a little to keep up with her longer legs. Fuming in silence for a minute or so, she suddenly realised that she was going too fast for him.

She said a little sheepishly, 'Sorry,' and slowed up.

'Quite all right, my dear. You're very tall, aren't you?' He said it mildly.

'Damn it, Owen, did I do anything wrong?' Diana exploded suddenly.

'You handled things marvellously, my dear. You closed the meeting just when you should have. The devil of it is, I can't figure out why they didn't just call and cancel the meeting.'

'Did you see their faces, Owen? They were relieved when I got up to go. It was as if they'd been vague on purpose, and never intended to try to reach an agreement for a contract. They came here and didn't even try!'

'I wonder if they might have heard that the Pittsburgh workers were on strike. It's hard to imagine where they would have heard that, because we've kept it very quiet,' he mused. 'That's the only possible explanation I can think of that makes any sense.'

Diana rubbed her neck tiredly. The rest of the day seemed to suddenly become a burden that she didn't want to carry. She said her goodbyes to Owen as he reached his floor, and continued up to the top floor. When she reached the offices, she poured herself a cup of coffee and collapsed on the couch in Carrie's room, smiling twistedly at the other woman.

Carrie turned off her typewriter and asked, 'How did things go in the meeting?'

'Pretty bad,' Diana replied. 'They didn't even want to come to an agreement. The only thing Owen and I can figure out is that they somehow got wind of the strike in Pittsburgh and they're afraid we won't be able to make shipments on time. Nothing else makes any sense.'

'Alex is going to be livid,' Carrie stated with conviction, 'absolutely livid! I wouldn't be surprised if he never worked with Nelson again. They never did like each other very much. Roger Nelson is an old man who inherited the business and who'll give it to his son to inherit. Alex, to them, is just a cocky upstart who never belonged in the élite group of aristocratic businessmen in the first place. They always resented the way Alex was able to make Peter Jackmon's dying business a highly powerful company. Of course, Peter Jackmon was their friend and neighbour, which didn't help matters at all.'

Diana whistled. 'There's a lot of history involved in this that I didn't know about, then.'

'Oh, yes. In a way it's almost comical. All the businessmen's wives and daughters absolutely love Alex, and all the businessmen—at least, the ones who are envious of Alex's ability—hate him.'

'And how does Alex feel?'

'Oh, Alex loves the ladies. As for the businessmen, he couldn't care less. He appreciates it when they avoid him. He never could stand incompetence.' Carrie smiled as she spoke.

Diana groaned as she got up from the couch. 'Lord, my head hurts! Will this day never end? I suppose it's back to the grindstone again.'

As she reached the door, Carrie spoke behind her. 'Why don't you make an early day of it today, Diana? You've been here early and gone home late for the past few days.

Surely things can hold off until tomorrow, if you leave around four, can't they? I'll take care of locking up the office for you.'

Diana turned. 'That sounds really tempting. I'll think about it and let you know, okay? I want to see how fast I can get through the pile of stuff on my desk.'

In the end Diana did go home early. The drive home was accomplished in a hazy daze. She was too tired to even care when the traffic got maddeningly slow, or stopped altogether. She simply sat quietly until it was her turn to go. When she got home and let herself into the apartment, she took enough time to make a broccoli casserole to pop in the oven. Then she set her alarm and fell into bed to sleep until her dinner was done.

The ringing went on and on and on . . . Diana jumped out of bed and, realising it was the phone, made a grab for the receiver.

'Hello,' she sighed.

'You were asleep, weren't you?' Alex accused. 'This is the second time I've woken you up. Considering that I've only called you twice so far, that's a pretty high average.'

'It also isn't an accurate average, since you've only called twice!' she retorted.

'I'll have to keep track of my calls and your naps, then, to get an accurate estimate of how much time you spend in bed.' He chuckled deeply.

She cleared her throat. 'This,' she said severely, 'can't possibly be the reason why you called, can it?'

'No, Madam Dragon, it isn't.'

'Madam Dragon!' Diana exclaimed, giving up all hope of ever getting Alex out of his teasing mood. 'Is that how you see me?'

'My dear, you might blush if I told you how I see you right now.' His voice had a definite note of amusement in it, and Diana felt a warmth on her cheeks, but forbore to tell him she was blushing anyway. He continued, 'I talked with Owen just a few minutes ago. He told me about the meeting this morning.'

'I'm sorry about the contract,' she apologised.

'Don't be,' he spoke crisply. 'I've a feeling that we're better off without it. Nelson's an old lady.'

'We thought that the only logical explanation would be if they heard about the strike and wanted to push us into breaking relations with them,' Diana told him. 'We just couldn't figure out who told them about the strike, because so few know about it. How are things in Pittsburgh?'

He replied with enthusiasm, 'I got everything worked out this afternoon. They start back to work in the morning!'

'That's terrific!' she exclaimed.

'Terrific as far as production goes,' Alex replied hardly. 'The whole thing looks as if it was rigged, except I could have sworn that those strikers were really worried. Now what I'm trying to find out is who would want to set me up?'

'Can you think of somebody in particular?' she asked quietly.

'I can think of quite a few people. I just have no way of proving it.'

'What are you going to do about it?'

'Come home. Will you meet me at the airport tomorrow morning at nine o'clock?' At her affirmative, he continued, 'Good girl! I'm glad to be coming home. Did you miss me?'

Searching for just the right note of light amusement, Diana was pleased with her reply. 'Of course. I had a hard time filling in for you. Your shoes were too big for me!'

He sighed. 'That's what I was afraid of. I bet nobody missed me. Everyone was probably glad to have me gone.' Pathos oozed from his self-pitying tone.

She laughed at him. 'I think you're nothing but a dramatist!'

He sounded offended. 'I beg your pardon!'

They rang off after a few more minutes, and Diana went to take her casserole out of the oven with a lighthearted feeling. It would be good to see him again, she thought to herself. She searched her mind in an effort to understand just why it would be nice to see Alex. It was an odd feeling, one she had seldom felt before, this active desire to see someone else. Alex had such a charisma about him, an indefinable charm that made her laugh. He appealed to her sense of humour. She appreciated his wit. She marvelled at how compatible they both seemed to be, and how quickly a working relationship between them had been established.

It felt like such a luxury to sit down at a supper before eight o'clock. Diana lingered over her meal and read the paper. Then she made a pot of hot tea and went into the living room in her dressing gown to watch television. There was a good mystery movie on and she enjoyed the suspense, the pleasurable tingle of fear that it gave her.

When ten o'clock rolled around, she was still feeling alert and restless, so she locked up the apartment and went downstairs to the old double garage that Terry, Brenda and she used for storage. She unlocked the side door and, walking in, brought out a slim, gleaming bicycle. She climbed on it and wheeled out of the driveway.

The wind whistled through her hair and she cycled down the street. The whole night was restless, the trees swaying and clouds gliding as the wind prowled the night. A half-moon gave a pearly glow to the quiet streets. Diana could hear dogs barking some distance away. She continued for about an hour or so, until she started to feel a little winded. Then she turned for home again, always

taking side streets and winding roads, searching for soli-
tude, until she finally ended up back at the old garage. By
now, she was exhausted, and she thankfully climbed the
stairs to go into her apartment, kick off her shoes, and get
ready for bed. She felt her muscles relax slowly under the
soothing warmth of her blankets. This time she had a
peaceful night.

The next morning she got out of bed feeling refreshed
and relaxed. Not being a morning person, she felt sure it
had quite a bit to do with the extra hour of sleep, and not
getting up at five o'clock. She showered and put on her
make-up before going to start some coffee. Then she went
to pick out something to wear. The past few days she had
worn skirt sets, but today she reached for a black pair of
slacks and waistcoat with a shimmery white shirt-blouse
that had a ridiculously extravagant bow on the neck. The
frilly blouse brought a relief to the very plainly cut pants
and waistcoat, and when Diana looked in the mirror, she
knew she looked good. Satisfied, she turned to pick up her
keys and bag and then left.

At the airport, she parked the car and went to find the
gate that Alex would disembark from. She had a few
minutes, so she took her time peering into a few shops and
watching the people. When she reached the gate, she had
a few magazines that she had purchased, tucking them
under her arm. She found a seat and started to leaf
through the magazines, and was halfway through the
second one when she felt a slight tickling behind her ear.
Reaching up, she tried to brush it away, but it came back,
this time a little stronger. She turned her head.

'Alex! How long have you been standing there?'

He was bigger and more handsome than she remembered, she thought as he replied lazily, 'Only for a moment. I just had enough time to tickle your neck.'

Diana got up in one swift motion, her body fluid and

graceful. Alex watched her move. She said, 'It's good to see you. Do you want to go straight to the office, or would you like to stop by your apartment first?'

'Neither one. I'm famished, girl! I think we should go and get something to eat first of all,' Alex grumbled, raking his hand through his hair, making it wavy and chaotic.

She laughed, 'Didn't you eat breakfast?'

Cocking an eyebrow at her, he replied, 'Of course. But that was hours ago. Everything I ate has been digested.'

She made a face. 'How horrible! I guess we'd better do something about it, since you're so obviously dying of starvation.'

He winced. 'Oh, sarcasm! Now she really is disgusted with me!'

'I am not, so quit playing the pathetic role. You'll get no sympathy from me,' she told him.

They reached the car and got in, Alex holding the door for her, before getting in himself. They went to a delightful little breakfast place that Alex knew of and ate mushroom omelettes with cheese, and some delicate pastries afterwards, and drank far too much coffee. They talked about everything: Diana told him about her trip to Italy, Alex spoke of England and his stay there several years ago, and they both shared college experiences. Alex delighted her with several stories of his madcap adventures with one of his college buddies. She didn't believe half of what he told her.

He seemed offended. 'You really don't believe me, do you?'

'No, I don't,' she laughed, leaning back in her chair. He watched her face and its changing expressions with apparent fascination.

'What is it you don't believe?' he asked. A smile tugged at the corner of his mouth. 'I can prove it, all of it!'

'Well, for one thing, I don't believe you took all the laboratory rats from the psychology department and put them in the women's dorm!'

'We did! I swear it!'

'—or that you would be cruel enough to jam the doors from the outside, so that the poor girls couldn't get out!' Diana accused him. They were laughing hysterically, and he sat there, holding his sides, and shook.

'And when they finally got the doors open, the girls had to sweep the rats out with brooms!' Alex howled, covering his face with one hand.

'Rats all over the campus!' gasped Diana, tears streaming from her face as she tried to control her laughter.

Their waitress walked by them to another table, giving each of them a strange look, almost as if she was half offended at the thought of anyone being so disgustingly cheerful in a public place. They managed to compose themselves as Alex paid the bill and went to leave the tip, but as they walked out of the restaurant, they both still had fits of uncontrollable mirth.

They then stopped by his apartment so that Alex could shower and change before going to the office. He showed Diana around the place before disappearing into the bathroom. 'Feel free to wander where you like,' he told her, 'as long as you don't wander around in my bedroom when I'm about through with my shower, otherwise you might see something you'd wish you hadn't.' His eyes danced.

Diana said dryly, 'Don't worry about me. I'll keep myself busy in your living room, looking at your books.'

As she strolled over to look at his book collection, she was pleased to see a great variety of books including several classics, quite a few current best-sellers, a little science fiction and fantasy, and a collection of mysteries. It revealed a little of Alex's personality in that he was well rounded and versatile in his tastes. She picked up a book that she hadn't seen before and started to leaf through it. Putting it back on the shelf, she had moved to the curtained windows when she heard the bathroom door open and the heavy tread of Alex's footsteps in the hall.

'Would you mind if I opened the curtains to look out of the window?' she called over her shoulder. Catching a glimpse of blue, she turned to see him walking casually into the room in a short terry-cloth robe that showed a great deal of muscular, hairy legs. Trying to appear as casual as Alex, she looked back to the window and away from the sight of him.

'Of course not,' he replied. 'I certainly think we're high enough so that no one can peek in if they wanted to.' The apartment was located at the top of a high-rise apartment building. Only three apartments were on this floor, and Diana was secretly impressed when she'd found out that a separate elevator was used by the top floor tenants only.

As she pulled the curtain cord, she became aware of Alex standing right behind her and looking over her shoulder. Afterwards, she couldn't remember how she knew that he was there, for he never touched her in any way. Some sixth sense warned her and she looked back over her shoulder at him.

'It's a beautiful view, isn't it?' he said softly as he looked out over the city. 'At night I can almost feel as if I'm on top of a mountain looking out over all of civilisation, just watching the lights winking and blinking all through the night.' He smiled a wry, twisted smile as he glanced down at her still and listening face. 'Of course all I have to do is to look up around me at the walls of my apartment confining me and the illusion is lost. But sometimes I don't look around me.'

Diana looked back over the city and imagined what it would feel like to be on a mountain. She said flatly, 'I can't picture it. I've never been on top of a mountain in my entire life. This has got to be the highest I've ever been, except for flying in a plane, and I've always taken afternoon flights.'

Alex shook his head. 'Honey, have you missed out on a lot of living! There's nothing like the feel of climbing your last, dirty, aching tired step to stand up and look over all you've climbed and attained. The view is best when you have to sweat for it.'

Diana laughed lightly and swung away from the window to go and sit on the comfortable sofa. She shook her head at him as she scoffed, 'Men! They're all alike. Why do men like to climb mountains so much? I think it has something to do with the macho image that all men think they have to project for all females!' She chuckled as she teased him.

He began to smile at her sexist remarks. 'There are plenty of women mountain climbers, you know, and not every man likes that particular challenge. Besides, haven't you climbed your own personal mountain, attained your own personal goal when you qualified for your degree? It's the same thing.'

'Whoa!' she held up her hands as she stopped Alex's flow of words. 'You, sir, are getting entirely too symbolic for this conversation. No—all right, I take back the "sir." But what I'd like to know is what happened to our light and meaningless conversation when I was being a chauvinistic and sexist pig? Now, that was fun.'

Alex was laughing at her as she spoke. 'That's what I like—a female chauvinist,' he chuckled. 'Makes a nice change from the usual.'

As he turned to go to his room to change, the telephone rang. Stopping in midstride, he swivelled to walk back to the coffee table where the phone was and picked it up.

'Alex Mason,' he said shortly. Diana looked at the

expression on his face as he listened and was alarmed to see his face change, grow harder, and his eyebrows came down into a thunderous frown.

'When?' he snapped. There was a short pause while he listened to the other person on the phone, then he replied, 'I'll be right there,' and hung up.

They looked at each other from across the room. She asked, 'Trouble?' He nodded.

CHAPTER THREE

ALEX and Diana broke the speed limit in their haste to reach the office. On the way, he told her what little was told to him by Carrie, who had been the caller.

'Apparently the Philadelphia foundry was nearly burned down last night. Arson is the cause. If it hadn't been such a bungling attempt, the bastards just might have made it.' Alex spoke through clenched teeth. His face appeared to be all angles, and his skin was drawn tightly over the bone. Blue fire glittered in his eyes as he made an attempt to control his rage.

Diana was stunned. 'Why?' she whispered. 'Who would hate you or Mason Steel so much as to want to destroy a whole foundry?'

'God, I wish I knew,' he muttered. They had just pulled up into the parking lot of Mason Steel, and he sat with his hands still gripping the steering wheel, the knuckle bones showing white. 'It doesn't make any sense!'

She repeated his words as if they bothered her: '"Doesn't make any sense." Why would something like that happen if it doesn't make any sense? Why would the factory workers go on strike if it didn't have any sensible basis?'

Sitting very still, Alex looked as if he'd been hit. 'And why,' he concluded, 'would Nelson's people refuse to deal with what should appear to be a firm and reliable business?' His eyes narrowed. 'Everything is so illogical until you put it all together. Then a very ugly pattern starts to emerge. It could all be on purpose. But that leads us back to—why?'

They both got out of the car, moving absentmindedly as each mulled over the problem in their minds. 'It's like an attempted murder,' she shivered. Alex put his arm around her shoulders as they both walked towards the building.

Alex was thinking very hard. 'Murder,' he repeated, mulling over the word. 'Murder has a motive. Most murders are committed by people who knew their victim. Most are committed in a fit of passion.'

'Something this deliberate has to have a motive,' she agreed. As he removed his arm to open the glass door, she preceded him, still talking. 'Could revenge be the motive?'

Shaking his head, he replied, 'I've done nothing to anyone aside from taking away a few customers from Derrick Payne, the other big steel manufacturer in this part of the country. God knows he has no reason to love me for it, but revenge? I'd say that's a bit strong.'

'Strike revenge. How about fear?' she asked.

'Fear doesn't make any sense. Who would fear me? I'm not spiteful or cruel, and have no secrets in my sordid past to conceal.'

'Okay, so we scratch fear. What about hate?'

'Hate is an interesting emotion,' he said thoughtfully. 'There's such a fine line between hate and love, each bearing intense emotion, each directed to someone who is close or has been in the past. Once you pass that line between love and hate, there's no going back to the original emotion.'

By now they had reached the offices on the top floor. 'It's simple,' said Diana, going in through the door first again. 'There's no purpose to this madness. You and I are becoming paranoid. There is no diabolical hand in this mess-up, and Mason Steel is just having a bad week.'

'Now that's the most far-fetched of all the ideas,' he sighed. 'Murphy's law is not this bizarre.'

'So, where do we start over?' she spread her hands in

perplexity. She had suggested everything she could think of.

Alex shook his head and turned towards Carrie. She was seated behind her desk and turned an anxious face towards them. 'Anything new come up?' he asked quietly.

Carrie looked down at her memo pad and spoke. 'Mike Shubart called again to confirm that it was a professional arson attempt. If it hadn't been for Mike going back last night to pick up a jacket that he'd forgotten, the whole thing would be ashes right now.' She shook her head. 'Lady luck was with us last night.'

'I know, Carrie,' Alex replied. 'I know. Have they figured up how much damage was done?'

'It was pretty minimal, except for a few electricity circuits. They were damaged pretty badly. Also the telephones in the whole place are out. The fire burned the main lines. Mike said that the insurance agent will be going over tonight in the early evening to inspect the damages. He wanted to know if you could come over for the night and be there for when the agent comes. He also thought you would like to see for yourself what was done.'

'He's right, I would,' Alex affirmed. Blowing a soundless whistle for a moment as he thought, he came to a decision. 'Find out if you can get me a flight to Philadelphia by late afternoon. If you can't that soon, then we'll have to charter a plane. Also, get Owen on the phone for me. I want to talk to him. Diana—would you cancel any appointments that I have this afternoon and tomorrow morning? Use the phone in the room across the hall. After you've finished that, come back in here. We've got some planning to do.'

With those orders despatched, he pivoted on his heel and disappeared into the other room. Diana grabbed the appointments schedule and left Carrie beginning to dial her phone.

It took her several minutes to reach everyone on the schedule book. Afterwards, she went quickly back to the other offices. As she passed Carrie's desk, Carrie called to her, 'Tell him a plane is chartered for four-thirty this afternoon.'

Diana waved a hand and pushed the door open. Alex was still talking on the phone. '. . . I still think it's too crazy. She couldn't have that much feeling for somebody else,' he argued.

Diana went to her desk and set the appointments schedule down, and sat in her chair quietly waiting. She wondered who they were talking about. Alex listened for a few more minutes and then spoke again.

'Owen, she may be a bitch, but that doesn't mean she would be so malicious as to try a stunt like arson!' he snapped. Pausing to listen again, his eyes strayed to Diana's, but he was not seeing her. 'All right, I'll leave you to look into it. I'll give you a call later.' He hung up.

'Does Owen think he's got a possibility for who could have done it?' she asked. Alex's eyes focused on her and he was silent for a moment.

'He seems to think so,' he replied shortly. 'Personally, I don't think Alicia feels anything for anyone but herself. I can't see how she could care to do something so vengeful.'

Diana prudently said nothing, and after a little silence, Alex became brisk. 'Did Carrie manage to get me a flight?' he asked.

'She chartered a plane for you for four-thirty,' she replied.

He looked at the clock. 'Well, that doesn't leave much time for us to get everything done, does it? Let's get started with the price estimates.'

They worked quickly and efficiently, each already used to the other's method of thinking, and each complimenting the other's output. Alex's mind worked so fast that Diana was tasked to the utmost of her ability, but she somehow managed to keep up with his pace, although realising that it was a pace that she could not sustain for long.

They did not break for lunch, but worked on through the afternoon until three-thirty. Then, flexing his cramped shoulder muscles, Alex called a halt.

'I need to go and throw a few things in my overnight case,' he sighed. 'You can leave whenever you finish plotting that chart for our accountants.'

Looking up, Diana asked, 'Do you need a ride to the airport again?'

'Thanks, no. I'm going to drive my own car to the apartment and get a taxi to the airport,' he replied. 'You have enough to do with that on your desk as it is. However, I might like to be picked up tomorrow whenever I get back. Could you do that?'

'Sure,' she affirmed. 'Just call me tomorrow at my apartment or later on at work, and let me know when.'

'Sounds good. I'm going to take off now. I don't think you'll be able to reach me at the factory, because the lines are out, but I'll call and leave my hotel number.'

She nodded; it was what she had expected. She only hoped that nothing would happen while he was at the foundry. Alex stood looking at her with a strange expression on his face, studying her with an odd intensity, while she sat with her head bent over the chart. He sighed heavily, and she looked up, but now he was gazing out of the window.

'I hate to go, to always be leaving,' he said in a low voice. She sat very still and listened. 'Very soon, I'm going to be slowing down a little, taking things a little easier. For nine years I've been rushing around like a cat with his tail on fire, never stopping, never slowing, always pushing to meet *this* deadline and get ahead on *that* one. Diana,' he shook his head at her, 'I've had it. This is how people get ulcers and high blood pressure and have heart attacks while they're still young. Maybe I just had to prove something, prove that I could win against the odds, make my own fortune. Now, I'm just tired.' He put his hands up to the back of his neck and rubbed.

Diana put her hands on her desk and looked at them. Wasn't that how they all were? Racing around, always proving something, always looking to the goals ahead and the achievements to be, never savouring the moment that is. Time, she thought, I've wasted so much time. She looked up at Alex and her vision was blurred.

Alex was horrified to see the unnatural glitter of tears in Diana's eyes. He looked away and spoke lightly to give her time to get control of herself again, 'When I get back from Philadelphia, we're going to have a picnic somewhere in the woods, just you and I. We'll forget that Mason Steel, Pittsburgh, and Philadelphia even exist. All right?'

Sniffing a little, she threw her head back and laughed, albeit rather unsteadily. 'All right,' she agreed.

Swiftly glancing at the clock on his desk, he went over to her and kissed her on the forehead, saying, 'Be good. Call you tomorrow.'

'Yes.' She watched him leave.

Wanting to get her work done as soon as possible, she didn't stop at all, oblivious of the dimming of the afternoon light. She didn't hear the door open or the footsteps until Carrie spoke right by her shoulder.

'Coffee?' Carrie asked. Diana jumped, and Carrie laughed to see the expression on her face. Diana chuckled a little too.

'Sure, I'd appreciate it,' she acknowledged.

A few minutes later, Carrie was back in the room carrying two steaming cups. Handing one to Diana, she moved over to one of the armchairs, pulled it around, and sank down into it.

'Oh, that's nice,' Carrie sighed. She started to laugh. 'When I started to work here, it took me three weeks of telling myself that soon things would slow down to normal, before I realised that this *is* the normal!'

Diana smiled.

'Surely things aren't as hectic as this all the time?' she queried.

'No, really we have had a lot happen that normally doesn't. But Alex is simply too energetic to let things happen at a slower pace. If something isn't going on, he starts something else,' Carrie replied ruefully.

'I bet he'll be unbearable whenever he decides to retire, then!' Diana chuckled.

'Oh, he'd be the type that would drive his wife up the wall with too much energy and too little to do,' Carrie laughingly agreed. 'But Alex probably would be the kind that works until collapse. No inactivity for him!'

Diana nodded. That did sound like Alex, she thought. Then she remembered how tired Alex sounded when he talked to her before he left. She also remembered something else. 'Carrie, do you know a woman named Alicia?'

Carrie grimaced. 'Do I know Alicia!' she exclaimed. 'The only Alicia that I know is Alicia Payne, Derrick Payne's daughter. And if that's the one you mean, you don't want to know her!'

'That bad, huh?'

'Worse. This girl is the original blonde-haired, blue-eyed, hypocritical bitch.' Diana whistled, and Carrie continued, 'Alex used to date her from time to time, and she was always careful that he didn't see her temper, but I saw her get angry at a poor girl who spilled coffee on her skirt by accident.' She shuddered. 'She was so vindictive!'

'Alicia Payne,' Diana looked at the ceiling as she spoke. 'Her father is also in steel, isn't he?'

'Yes, although he really isn't much competition for us now. His company is smaller than ours and his output is less. I don't think he's very efficient, myself.'

'Do we have the potential ability to put him out of business if Alex wanted to?'

Carrie looked surprised. 'Why, I suppose we do, although Alex doesn't work like that.'

Diana looked at her. 'But old Derrick might think like that?'

A light began to gleam in Carrie's eyes. 'I believe he might at that. What are you thinking, Diana?'

'A motive,' she told her, 'for murder. The murder of Mason Steel. I take it that Alex is no longer seeing Alicia?'

'That's right. A few months ago, Alex told her he didn't want to see her again. Little Miss High and Mighty was getting a bit too possessive for her own status. She started demanding, expecting Alex to give in like I'm sure her daddy does for her.' Carrie rolled her eyes at Diana. 'She came storming out of Alex's office, eyes spitting venom, and we haven't seen her in here again, much to my delight.'

'All of the motives are there, Carrie!' Diana said excitedly. 'Do you see it? Fear, hate and revenge.' She ticked them off on her fingers as she spoke. 'Fear Derrick feels for Alex's growing power in his own line of business and his own inability to cope. Hate comes when you fear something as a direct threat to yourself. Also, I'm sure Alicia isn't feeling too friendly towards Alex right now. And revenge. Remember that old saying about a woman scorned? I think we can paraphrase it to make it fit our needs. How about "Hell hath no fury like a bitch who's scorned"? Nice, huh?'

'Oh, dear, do you really think they would?' Carrie asked doubtfully.

She shrugged. 'I don't know. I couldn't be sure until I met them both and found out for myself how they really are. I overheard Alex talking to Owen, and Owen seems to think so! Anyway, there's nothing we can do about it for tonight, so the only thing I'm going to do is go home to bed. I can ask Alex about it tomorrow,' she finished.

Carrie took out the used Styrofoam cups while Diana began to tidy up the office. She turned off the light when she was through, and locked the door. On her way out, she stopped at Carrie's desk.

'How long do you plan on staying, madam?' she asked.

Carrie smiled as she looked up. 'I think I'll stay for another fifteen minutes or so, until I finish up these two business letters.'

'Is it all right if I leave you to finish the locking up, then?'

'Of course. Please don't stay around here if that's all you need to do,' she replied. She smiled warmly up at Diana.

'Then I'll say goodnight,' Diana smiled back as she took her leave and left the office.

On her way down to the main floor, she stopped to drop off the chart that she had completed to the third floor where the accountants were, then hurried out of the building. She got into her little sports car and backed out of her parking space.

Diana felt uneasy as she drove home. Fear, she thought as she carefully made a turn, revenge and hate. All of them were intense emotions, and she felt uncertain of the conclusions that she had so blithely drawn in the office when she was talking to Carrie. She did not know either Alicia or Derrick Payne. All she had to go on was a half-heard conversation that Alex had with Owen, and

Carrie's own opinion of Alicia Payne. Part was gossip and the other part was incomplete. By the time Diana had reached home, she had successfully talked herself out of believing that anyone had such a malicious intent towards Mason Steel. Feeling a little foolish, she resolved not to talk about it to anyone else.

There was another car pulled up by the kerb as Diana reached home, and she was delighted to see that Terry and Brenda were back home from their trip. She ran lightly up the front porch steps to knock on their door. Brenda answered it, a wide grin on her face as she saw who was at the door.

'Hello, strangers,' Diana exclaimed.

'Hello, yourself,' Brenda retorted. She held the door open wide and motioned with her hand. 'Don't just stand there gawking, girl, come on in!'

Diana stepped through the doorway.

'When did you get back?' she asked, waving at Terry as he passed by the doorway going down the hall. He rolled his eyes as he braked suddenly and came back to talk to her.

'All of fifteen minutes ago, wasn't it, hon?' Terry passed his arm around Brenda's waist.

'You idiot!' she pushed him away as she smiled, and turned to Diana. 'Don't believe a word of it! We've been home for at least three hours!' Diana began to laugh at the look of injured hurt on Terry's face.

He said stiffly, 'Just because I happen to be an inaccurate judge of time, she calls me an idiot!' Sticking his nose up in the air, he marched out of the room.

Diana, still chuckling, turned towards Brenda. 'What plans do you have made for supper?'

'We were just going to have sandwiches and soup,' Brenda replied. She continued hopefully, 'Unless you want to invite us over?'

'I was thinking that maybe we could combine suppers. I'll make a chicken casserole if you'll bring a salad, or something,' Diana offered.

'Great!' Brenda said enthusiastically. 'We'll bring our deck of cards, too. After supper we can play a few games.'

'All right. How about around six-thirty?' suggested Diana. She was secretly relieved that she didn't have to spend another night all alone in the house.

'Will do. See you then.'

They had a wonderful time that evening. Terry made an unexpected trip to the store and returned with a bottle of wine to top off the meal. Then they spent a hilarious evening playing all sorts of card games, and making up their own rules as they went along. As Terry put it, they were being innovative and creative. 'After all, the rest of the world just plays by somebody else's rules,' he explained haughtily.

All the same, Diana wondered what it would be like to have a foursome. More specifically, she wondered what it would feel like to have a partner, someone to team up with in games, someone to take your side in trouble, someone to go home with at night. She felt a great affection for Terry and Brenda and wished them all the happiness in the world, but at the same time they made her feel something was missing in her life. They were a team, while she had no one but herself. She didn't like to spend a great deal of time with them.

All three of them had to get up for work the next morning, so Terry and Brenda left fairly early after helping Diana clear up the supper mess and do the dishes.

After they left, Diana decided to go out biking. As she locked her apartment door, she assured herself that it was merely a physical tension she wanted to dispel. She tried not to think of her cold and empty bedroom. Wheeling down the driveway, she turned for the country roads, pedalling fast.

Terry and Brenda were in their darkened bedroom when they heard the sounds of the garage door being opened. Brenda padded to the window and peeped through. 'She's leaving again,' she said worriedly. 'I always feel anxious when she goes out at night like this.'

'She'll be all right,' Terry said soothingly. 'This is a nice neighbourhood, and it's quiet. She's always been all right in the past.'

'All the same, I don't like it,' Brenda replied sharply. 'I wish she wouldn't do it.'

'Can you blame her?' he asked quietly as he went over to the bed and pulled back the covers. 'She has nothing in that apartment to make her want to stay. And nobody to make her care to.'

Brenda turned from the window and her eyes rested on him. 'I suppose so . . .'

Diana, unaware of the discussion going on about her, sped on down the streets while visions of Mason Steel, and especially Alex, flashed through her mind. She shook her head angrily. I don't want to think about him! she told herself. I don't want to think . . . She thought of the short blue robe with muscled bare legs underneath, and her mouth went dry. A long steep hill lay before her and her mind accepted the challenge with relief.

By the time she reached home, she was physically and mentally exhausted. In the past she had been attracted to other men, but they had all been a sort of schoolgirl crush. Diana had realised early the nature of these crushes. She had known that they were unrealistic and fleeting. She also had realised that they were for her a form of escape when she was most weary. She had dimly envisaged a knight in shining armour who would come and carry her away from all of the unpleasantness of life and all responsibility.

Now she looked upon her attraction to Alex with dismay. Diana didn't want all of those old feelings to come back; she regarded them as unhealthy, a threat to her strength of personality. She resolved to do what she had in the past: avoid the situation at all costs.

With that settled in her mind, Diana wearily went to bed.

The next morning, she got up early. She wanted to be at the office by eight to work a little on a few financial reports before Alex got back from Philadelphia. She remembered something he had said about having those done by the weekend, and today was Friday.

Dressing quickly, she thought again about how strange events had been lately at Mason Steel. Alicia Payne came to mind, and she wondered what kind of motive the other girl would consider strong enough reason for such an act of vengeance. Diana had never experienced any wrong horrible enough to want to revenge it. She couldn't fathom somebody else imbued with such spite. Therefore such a thing was not possible.

Diana reached Mason Steel with all her doubts diminished.

As she entered the office, she was greatly surprised to see Owen Bradshaw in Carrie's seat with the phone receiver in his hand. He looked at her over his glasses, but said nothing. There was a look of strain about his face that sat oddly on such plumpness. Feeling rather horrible with a sick foreboding of disaster, Diana forgot to take off her coat as she sank on to the couch to wait for him to finish the call. As he finished, he leaned back in his seat with a sigh. 'I can't get hold of Alex,' Owen said flatly.

'He must be at the factory, because he told me he would be either there or at the motel,' she mused out loud. 'Of course the phone lines are out at the factory, so you couldn't reach him there.' She looked at Owen and forbore to ask any questions, although her eyebrows went up a little. He smiled a twisted smile at the expression on her face.

'We have to find him, Diana,' he stated quietly. 'It's going to happen today.'

For some inexplicable reason the words sent a chill down her back. 'Why?' she asked. 'What's wrong? What's going to happen today?'

He stood up and walked heavily around the desk. 'I don't know what,' he spoke reluctantly, acting half ashamed at his admission. 'Things have been happening so quickly around here . . .' He broke off. Then, with a direct look into Diana's eyes, he asked, 'Have you ever been so sure of something that, even though you have no proof, no logical argument, nothing concrete or sane to hold on to, you still believe in it with every conviction you hold solid?'

Only half comprehending what Owen meant, she asked tentatively, 'Do you mean something like intuition?' He nodded, looking a bit relieved, and she replied, 'Yes, I think I know what you mean. What are you so sure of?'

After a moment he said heavily, 'Alicia Payne.'

Diana closed her eyes. Oh no, she thought. 'And you think something else is going to happen today,' she stated, rather than asked.

'Yes.' The unemotional reply held a powerful conviction. 'The Pittsburgh factory is behind schedule. The Philadelphia one is not producing, even though you and I know that the delay is very temporary. Alex is away, unable to make decisions, with no knowledge of the current events taking place today. We can't reach him at the motel. The best time for another blow to Mason Steel is today, this morning. If there's somebody behind this, they'll know when to strike.'

Diana was thinking rapidly. 'Did you try sending someone in Philadelphia to the factory to try and locate Alex?'

'I tried that about twenty minutes ago. We should hear from him soon if they found him.' Owen shook his head. 'I'm going back down to my office. Let me know if you hear anything.'

'I will,' she promised as she walked him to the door. 'Owen?' He looked at her questioningly. She asked hesitantly, 'What do you think they'll do?'

'I don't know, my dear. I don't know.'

Concentrating was hard after the curiously intense meeting with Owen. His belief that Alicia Payne was capable of such maliciousness had shaken Diana's little delusion that she had fed last night when she had tried to convince herself that such vengefulness did not exist. She fidgeted around the office, wishing the phone would ring. It was crazy, she thought as she gazed out the window into the bright, sunny morning. I'm really a part of this team, and it all happened so quickly. I care what happens to Mason Steel, to Alex's company. I'm sweating along with everyone else. As she thought this, she suddenly realised how Mason Steel had occupied her thoughts, to the exclusion of everything else since she had started work. Nothing else in her life seemed quite as important anymore to her. All her concentration was centred on something beside herself for the first time in her life.

Carrie arrived, and Diana told her in an outpouring of words of Owen's conviction and their dread of what the morning would bring. Carrie merely nodded her head with no surprise.

'I don't find it hard to believe,' she said, when asked by Diana. 'I've met Alicia, and you haven't. It makes a difference.'

Diana could only shake her head blankly, at a loss for words.

The shrill sound of the telephone in the other room made both women jump. They looked at each other silently. 'I hope it's Alex,' Diana whispered. 'I hope he shouts at us for being fools.' She moved quickly to the desk and picked up the receiver. At first she instinctively held the phone away from her ear, the noise was so loud. Then she was shouting back into the phone, 'Calm down, for God's sake! I can't understand you!'

'—it doesn't make any sense!' the voice on the other end was shouting back. There was a slight pause. 'Diana?'

'Yes, Neil.' Neil Stratton was the head accountant in their accounting department.

'Have you heard what happened yet? Payne lowered his price of steel this morning—it's down almost twenty-three per cent of what our prices are! Diana, he's starting a price war with us!' His voice was rising as he became more agitated. 'He's committing financial suicide! What in Hades' name are we supposed to do, Diana?'

After the first stunned moment when she heard his words, she began to think furiously, her mind working quickly and clearly. 'Neil—listen to me! I'm going to call Alex and ask him what we need to do, and I'll be right down. In the meantime, you and the others start figuring out how much we can afford to knock off our prices without going under. Figure it down to the bare minimum. If Payne wants a price war, then that's what he's got to expect. Be right there.' She hung up without listening for a goodbye.

For a moment she simply sat there, her body motionless as her mind continued to race frantically. She then called for Carrie, telling her to try and reach Alex. 'Don't stop trying. We've got to find out where he is,' Diana told her. 'I'll be leaving to go down to Owen's floor, and then to the accounting department. Send the call through to me if you reach him.' Carrie hurried back to her office and Diana picked up her own phone. She looked around for the phone booklet; she had a few calls to make too.

Fifteen minutes later, Diana walked into Owen's office. He looked up from the jumbled pile on his desk. Sitting back, he immediately asked, 'Have you got in touch with Alex?'

Sighing, she replied, 'No.'

'I suppose you've tried to get in touch with the vice-president, Jim Marshall?' Owen looked down at his hands as he spoke. There was little hope in his voice, for the vice-president of the company was a mere figurehead, a title bestowed on an incompetent who earned the seat on the board of directors of Mason Steel by virtue of his large share of stocks in the company. He was invariably absent from the day-to-day working at Mason Steel, a fact that in the past had brought many sighs of relief from Owen and Alex, and showed up rarely at any of the board meetings. He was usually away on some fishing trip, out in the obscure reaches of the wilderness with no modern conveniences and no troublesome phones.

She slumped in her chair. 'Yes,' she sighed again. 'He's away. Some new fishing spot, Mrs Marshall said. He'll be gone for weeks.' Diana had never met Jim Marshall.

Owen was savage. 'We don't even have a figurehead of authority to work with!'

She was invaded with a sense of panic. Something had to be done right away, or Mason Steel could be ruined beyond repair. Derrick Payne's move had been a dead giveaway as to who had been the culprit behind the disasters at both of the steel factories. His company was smaller than Mason's, therefore his output was smaller. There was no chance in the world for Payne to win a price war under normal operating circumstances, for Mason could afford to cut their prices far lower than Payne could. It was, as Neil had exclaimed, financial suicide for Payne. However, one factory was behind schedule at Mason Steel, and the other, as far as Payne knew, was damaged if not destroyed beyond repair. With Mason's output cut drastically, Payne could deliver the final crippling blow to the company by cutting prices Mason could no longer afford to cut, creating panic selling of the Mason Steel stocks. Diana knew that she was envisaging the ruin of Alex's company if something wasn't done soon.

'Owen,' she said urgently, 'you've got to help me. We've got to tell everyone what Alex wants us to do, and it's got to be done right away, now, this morning, before we lose any more money. There's only one thing we can do—Payne has left us no choice. We have to cut our prices lower than his, and maintain our present output, God knows how. Get Jack Dobson on the phone and explain to him what's going on. They're going to have to work overtime until the Pittsburgh factory is back on its feet. After that, meet me down in the accounting department. I think that I'm going to need you to help me convince them that the price change is exactly what Alex has told us to do. It's the only thing we can do.'

He nodded. 'I know, Diana. I just hope we can convince them of that.' He picked up his receiver as she headed out of the door. 'Diana.' His voice stopped her as she put her hand on the doorknob. She turned enquiringly. 'I hope you're a good liar. I hope we're very good liars.'

She said soberly, 'I just hope that Alex agrees with what we're about to do. If he's angry, then I take full responsibility.'

She was out of the door and gone.

The accounting people were a little sceptical at first, but the habit of taking orders from someone in authority dies hard in some, and Diana and Owen represented the authority. Besides which, they both lied with an excellent show of credibility. Diana insisted on doing most of the talking with Owen only backing her from time to time, adding his own considerable influence only when the most reluctant balked. She was determined that nobody but her was going to get the blame for what she had decided. Owen, at first trying to reassure her that what they did was the only thing that they could do, later became nervous himself when Alex's plane arrived in New York that afternoon. Diana was unable to come to the phone when Alex called and when she learned that he had arrived at the airport, was quite alarmed at the thought of picking him up. In the end, Owen offered to go for her and pick Alex up himself, taking pity on her agitated state. She gratefully accepted.

'However,' she told a sympathetic Carrie, 'this only postpones the inevitable meeting. Oh, Carrie, I hope what we did was right!'

CHAPTER FOUR

DIANA sat back in her chair and rested her head tiredly. After staring at the ceiling for a few moments, she closed her eyes. Alex is going to be here any minute, she thought to herself. He's going to roar at me, tell me what a stupid fool I am, tear my ego to little tiny bits, and then fire me. She got a morbid sense of satisfaction out of thinking about it. It's either that, or promote me, she told herself, and smiled at the thought.

She had been so engrossed with herself, she didn't hear the door open to admit a very quiet Alex. His footsteps were nearly noiseless on the carpet, but some sixth sense made her look up calmly. Alex walked over to his own chair behind his desk and sank into it, one hand going up to rub his eyes which, even to Diana across the room, looked red-rimmed and tired.

'Hi,' she said softly. He turned his head and glanced at her. 'Are you going to fire me?' It was asked in a matter-of-fact way, almost cheerfully, as if it didn't matter at all.

One side of Alex's mouth curved upward. 'No, I'm not going to fire you, you little idiot.' Diana's back relaxed and she sagged in her chair, relieved. His gaze sharpened at the movement and he asked incredulously, 'Did you really think I would?'

She shrugged, a small movement of the shoulders, trying to seem unconcerned. Alex was watching her face. 'I didn't know what to expect, I guess,' she watched the ceiling as she spoke. 'To me, I couldn't see any other action to take; it was the only thing we could have done. But I didn't know if it was what you wanted to do.' She rolled her head a little on the chair. 'I didn't know if you wanted to resolve it another way.' I didn't know if you wanted to talk to Alicia instead, she thought, but didn't have the courage to say.

His face hardened. 'What else could I have done?' he asked sharply. 'Go to them and ask them if they might change their minds, maybe reconsider?' Diana winced at his tone. 'No, there was nothing else to do but that. Now we can only wait and see who cracks under the strain first, Payne or us. I only hope that the Pittsburgh plant can handle the extra work load until the Philadelphia plant is repaired. Otherwise Payne just might win.'

She moaned, 'I can just see it now. Late hours, hard work, no lunch breaks, no weekends relaxing at home . . .'

He continued the line of thought, '. . . no dinner dates, no days off, no theatre, no picnics until this is all resolved! Lord, it makes me tired just to think about it!'

Mason Steel had a hard time in the next few weeks. The Pittsburgh plant was worked to the limit, filling in for the Philadelphia plant, and also taking new orders for steel due to the price war that waged between Mason and Payne. Alex transported workers from Philadelphia to Pittsburgh so that the plant could be manned in three shifts until the other plant was operable. He was often gone from the New York offices to manage working conditions in Pittsburgh, and from time to time to check up on repairs in Philadelphia. Diana was indeed promoted to the proud office of Operating Manager, a title which gave her authority to make decisions in case she was unable to get in contact with Alex in case of emergency.

The price war was, in the meantime, waging strong. Payne lowered their prices two more times, but each time Mason Steel was able to beat them with even lower prices.

Diana, becoming too tired to commute from her apartment to the New York office, began to stay in Alex's
apartment at his insistence while he was away. She was
too tired to even feel nervous about the situation or to care
if he were to come home unexpectedly. She was working
an average of twelve hours a day, and sometimes more
than twelve, so when she finally got to the apartment she
barely took time to strip off her clothes before she fell into
bed. It was a big relief when Alex called her one night to
let her know that the repairs on the Philadelphia plant
were finished, and that it should be producing normally
within the next three days. That meant that he should be
home and able to take over most of the decision-making
within the next week. Diana felt a surge of triumph at his
words. With the Philadelphia foundry back in operation,
there was no doubt. Mason Steel could beat Payne at the
price war.

Diana made a mental note to herself, as Alex was
talking, to be out of his apartment in the next few days.
That way, she would be able to avoid any unforeseen
contact with him and keep things on a comfortable and
businesslike basis. Circumstances had been a little unusual, but in a short time things would be back to normal.
She hung up at the end of the conversation, telling herself
that she was only pleased that he was coming home so
that he could take some of the work load off of her
hands. However, that did not account for her ridiculously
happy feeling whenever she thought about seeing him
again.

The next day, she left work to go to Alex's apartment for
the last time. She was too tired to pack her few odds and
ends that night, so she went to bed promising herself that
the next morning she would put her things into her
overnight case and be gone by the time Alex would be
back. As she stood in the spare bedroom she'd been using,

she flexed her shoulders tiredly. She had put in another twelve hours today and she was beginning to feel the strain. I can't keep this up much longer, she thought. Alex, please come home. She crawled into bed slowly, falling asleep almost before her head hit the pillow.

A sound woke her up. She lay in bed frowning sleepily into the darkness, trying to figure out what had woken her. Then she heard a door somewhere in the apartment close softly. It was a small and furtive movement, as if someone was trying to make as little noise as possible. As if, Diana thought, somebody knew she was there . . . Alex. Alex was back before he had planned.

'Oh, blast it!' she muttered, throwing off her covers with exasperation. She would never sleep until she'd found out for sure if it was Alex or not, which meant a meeting that she had wanted to avoid. She put on her dressing gown and, belting it tightly around her waist, went out into the living room. The lamp by the couch was turned on, a soft and mellow light which nonetheless made her blink. She ran a hand through her hair impatiently to get it out of her eyes. Alex was standing with his back to the hallway, over by the bookcase pouring himself a drink of whisky. He had on a white shirt with the sleeves rolled up to the elbows and dark pants which emphasised his lean height. Diana closed her eyes at the sight and tried to stifle a huge yawn.

'Good lord,' she mumbled around her hand as she covered her mouth and yawned anyway. 'Did you have to make so much racket?'

He spun around in surprise. 'I woke you? You must be a very light sleeper to hear the front door open from all the way down the hall.'

'There was so much noise it would have awakened the dead,' she stated clearly, then yawned hugely again. She went over to the nearest easy chair and sank into it, curling her feet up under herself. 'Elephants, that's what I thought you were, a herd of wild elephants tramping through the apartment.'

Alex grinned at her. He was so damned handsome, she despaired as she thought to herself. Why does he have to be so good-looking? He moved over to the couch and sat down with his drink in one hand. 'Wild elephants, huh?' he said with a chuckle. 'That's one way I've never heard myself described. I tried to be quiet.'

'I didn't really hear you until after I was awake anyway,' she said. Her eyes were watering from yawning so much and Alex was a blur across the room. 'What time is it, do you know?'

He consulted his watch. Dark hairs from his arm curled around the gold band. 'Almost three in the morning.'

'Three o'clock! And my alarm is set for six!' she moaned, huddled in the chair. 'Why did you get back so soon? Is something wrong?'

He took a drink of his whisky and set it down on a side table. There were lines on his face that hadn't been there before he left. He has had a rough time of it, too, she realised. She thought of all of the flights he had made in the past few weeks. He'd definitely had a harder time of it.

'Mike Shubart didn't really need my help in Philadelphia any more, and neither did Dobson in Pittsburgh. Tomorrow all the workers go back home to Philadelphia, and everything should be almost back to normal. I thought you needed my help more than anybody,' Alex said with a keen look at her face. She had shadows under her eyes, dark smudges that emphasised her large eyes and made her face look fragile and pale. Her posture in the chair suggested a great weariness and she seemed a little thinner. He looked almost angry, and she couldn't figure out why.

'I've done a good job,' she said defensively. 'Did someone tell you I hadn't? Did Owen tell you?' She sounded indignant. 'I wasn't needing help.'

'Owen didn't breathe a word to me,' Alex sighed. 'Don't you think I could tell how you were feeling when I talked to you over the phone?' He leaned forward, putting his elbows on his knees and holding his glass in both hands. She watched his profile, the strong nose and mouth and the jutting outline of his cheekbone. He looked up suddenly, catching her eyes. 'I knew you had to be putting in at least ten to twelve hours a day, just to keep up with all of the new contracts you were sending us so fast! You haven't taken a day off in weeks, have you?' She looked away with a vague expression on her face. 'Have you?' he insisted, prompting a reluctant shake of the head.

'Well, have you taken a day off?' Diana was stung into asking.

He made an impatient gesture, jeopardising the safety of the drink he still held. 'I knew it!'

'It's different for me!' he said angrily. 'I can take it.'

She began to seethe inside, all traces of sleepiness gone. 'And I can't, is that it? Have I done such a bad job? Have I complained, or shirked some job that needed to be done? Have I?'

'That's not the point!' he snapped. 'I think you've done an excellent job with everything, and I know you haven't complained. I'm used to the long hours, though, and can take more than other people can.' He stood up and started to pace the room in impatient strides. 'And can you honestly say you could have handled the pace for very much longer?'

Diana remained silent, staring stonily at the floor in front of her. She was unprepared for the hand that came under her chin to tilt her head up. His hand and face were gentle and he said, 'I just didn't want to see you all worn out.' His face blurred to her as her eyes watered unexpectedly.

She tried to laugh and it came out shaky, as she wiped her eyes with both hands. 'I guess I'm more tired than I thought,' she sniffed. Her hands shook ever so slightly.

Alex took her hands and rubbed them for a moment. Then he suddenly let go and pulled her up with one arm around her waist. He kept his arm around her waist and walked her to the door of the spare bedroom, talking all the while. 'You're going to climb in bed right now, young lady, while I fix you a cup of hot chocolate. And you're not to get up in the morning, but you're going to sleep until you wake up by yourself. Then you're going to take the rest of the day off to spend it how you please. At five o'clock tomorrow afternoon you can meet me at the office, and we'll go out to dinner so you can fill me in on a few things. Okay?' He turned her around to face him and looked down at her with eyebrows raised.

She pleaded, 'Couldn't I come in just a little earlier to finish a contract propos—'

'No! That's an order, Diana. Don't you dare show your face before five o'clock!' He looked serious.

She chuckled a little. 'All right.'

He looked pleased with himself. 'Good girl! Now go and turn off your alarm and jump in bed. I'll be right back with your cocoa. Move, child!'

She looked indignant at that remark, but she scampered into bed quickly anyway. Soon he was back with the warm drink and he sat on the side of her bed and talked to her until she finished the relaxing drink. He then took the empty cup and watched her settle down in bed before he left the room. She was unprepared for the swift movement as he quickly bent down and brushed his lips against the top of her forehead and then was gone, closing the door behind him.

Going to sleep without the thought of the alarm going off was simply marvellous . . .

When Diana finally opened her eyes, daylight was seeping in through a crack between the curtains at the window. She turned her head lazily to the clock by the bed and sat bolt upright in bed. It was eleven-thirty in the morning! She had slept the whole morning away. Throwing off her covers and shrugging into her robe, she walked out into the hall and into the gleaming kitchen. There was a note on the table for her from Alex. It read: Dear Diana, if you show your face at the office before five, I'll beat you silly.

It was signed simply 'A'. She laughed when she read it and, folding it, carefully set it aside. After a quick cup of coffee and a nourishing breakfast of scrambled eggs and toast, she faced the perplexing problem of what to do with the rest of her day. What did one do with a free afternoon in the middle of New York City? She settled the problem in a typically feminine way: shop. Then she combed the streets of New York with nothing on her mind other than the delightful prospect of new clothes.

Hours later, she let herself into Alex's apartment laden down with packages. After kicking off her shoes and padding to the spare bedroom with her load, she set about opening her packages to lay out and take stock of what she had bought. The first package held a dark red sweater dress that clung to her figure lovingly to fall just below the knee. She set that aside; that was for the winter months, now coming up soon. Opening the next box, she pulled out a dusty black one-piece jumpsuit that zipped up the front and had tapering legs with a wide belt. She eyed it with some perplexity. It was a very chic outfit, figure-hugging and attractive, but she had no idea where she would wear it.

The last box was what she really wanted to look at. As

she opened the box, she couldn't resist the urge to try the dress on. Shaking it out, she once again felt the uncertainty she had experienced when the salesgirl had urged her to try the dress in the first place, for it seemed shapeless and unattractive in her hands, in spite of the delicately beautiful colour. It had several different shades of the palest lavender, the most delicate purple, and the most subtle blues that she had ever seen. It had frankly cost the earth. She handled the dress with gentle hands as she slipped it over her head. After zipping the almost invisible zipper in the back, she went over to the full-length mirror and surveyed herself. What bodice there was to the top was low and very tight with tiny straps for her shoulders. The skirt was four layers of very thin and very light material that slid sensuously around her hips and thighs as she had put it on, and seemed to float when she walked. The colour faded as it went down the skirt until it ended in transparent jagged edges that stopped at her lower calf, giving tantalising glimpses of her legs when she moved. The muted hues somehow transformed her facial colouring and hair. Her lips were more red, her eyes more vivid, and her hair had a higher gloss. It was a graceful dress, lending a fragility to her tall slimness that she had never known before.

After staring at herself for a long while, she finally took the dress off with a sigh. She would wear it at one of the formal parties that Alex had said would be coming up this autumn with her slender silver sandal shoes with the ridiculously high heels, and she would feel like a princess, regal and graceful, dancing the night away with a very tall, very big, dark man holding her close—she turned away from her thoughts with the desperation of one hunted. Suddenly becoming painfully brisk and businesslike, she set about packing her odds and ends quickly. She would not be coming back to the apartment tonight. She cleared up her shopping mess and picked up her toothbrush from the bathroom. She tried to feel happy about staying in her own apartment, but all she felt was emptiness.

When faced with the dilemma of changing for dinner, Diana happily got out her black jumpsuit and slid into its close-fitting length and zipped the zipper up. It stopped just above her bra, showing a suggestion of a shadowed cleft that was between her breasts. She started to put her hair up in its customary knot high on her head and stopped, deciding instead to let it swing free in a glossy full tumble down her back. She touched up her make-up, slipped on a pair of slender high-heeled black shoes, and picked up her suitcase to leave. Just inside the front door, she turned. Her gaze swept the spacious apartment with regret, and then she walked out the door.

The drive to Mason Steel was quick, and she locked her car in the parking lot. Then, moving swiftly towards the building, she reflected on how different everything would be now that Alex was back. She went into the building and quickly towards the elevator.

Minutes later, she walked into Carrie's office with a wide smile. She was pleased to see Carrie's face light up as she looked up to Diana.

'Why, hello!' Carrie exclaimed cheerfully. 'You look a lot better after having a little time off. You look as though you got a full night's sleep for a change!'

Diana laughed. 'I slept until eleven o'clock this morning!'

'It must be nice,' Carrie sniffed. 'I think the last time I slept in until eleven was the day after I gave birth to my youngest daughter, fourteen years ago!'

Diana shook her head at Carrie in disbelief. 'Now, I definitely don't believe a word of that!' Carrie started to chuckle too. 'Is Alex in?'

'Yes. He told me to tell you to go on in when you got here,' Carrie replied. 'Owen is in there right now, talking to Alex about something, but they won't mind if you go on in.'

'Thanks.' She walked to the other door and knocked lightly before walking in. Alex was in his customary leaning posture against the front of his desk and Owen was perched on the arm of one of the chairs facing him. Both men looked up when she entered.

'Speak of the devil!' Owen exclaimed with a grin. 'How are you doing?'

'I'm glad you weren't speaking of me,' she said demurely, surprising them both into chuckling. 'I'm just fine. Those extra hours of sleep did wonders!'

Alex ran an appreciative eye over her as she walked towards them, but made no comment on how she looked. She felt vaguely and unreasonably let down as if she had expected him to compliment to her, since she knew she looked good.

He spoke. 'We're going to wait for Grace Bradshaw to come, if you don't mind. Owen and Grace are going to dinner with us.'

She said warmly, 'Now, why in the world should I mind?' She turned to Owen. 'Ever since you told me about your wife, I've been longing to meet her.' Owen looked pleased. One day, a few weeks ago, he had described his wife to Diana with so much love and pride, it had brought a lump to her throat. She was a frail woman, he had told her, obviously concerned, and she fought a constant battle with asthma, one that left her physically weak and drained.

They all three talked for a few minutes more, then left for the first floor to meet Grace there. Once there, Owen gave an exclamation and hurried away to meet a small and delicately boned woman with a beautiful head of silvery white hair that was swept up in a simple style.

Diana, feeling like a horse beside a small gazelle, shook her head ruefully and murmured, 'Not a bit like me, is she?'

Alex had been watching the two approach and he turned his head sharply, catching the faint words although Diana had not really meant him to. 'No, she isn't,' he said softly. 'She's tiny and delicate and she has to struggle for every breath she takes.' (. . . and she is loved and wanted and cared for as if she were something immeasurably precious, she thought.) 'No, you aren't a bit like her,' he twisted the words around. 'Thank God!'

The couple had reached Alex and Diana, and Owen proudly made the introductions between Diana and his wife. Now that Grace was closer, she could see the lines of pain that had marked the older woman's face deeply, scoring the skin around her eyes and mouth. Diana held out her hand and shook the other woman's gently. 'You're every bit as beautiful as Owen had described,' she said.

Grace's face lit up. 'How kind of you to say so, my dear, although I'm afraid I can't hold a candle to you.'

Diana started to walk to the front of the building with Grace. 'Now, that just isn't true!' she declared as she shortened her stride to match that of the smaller woman. They started chatting comfortably as if they had known each other all of their lives, unaware of the smiles the two men exchanged as they followed behind. When they reached the parking lot, it was decided that all three of the cars should be taken so that everyone could leave for home from the restaurant. Alex would take the lead to the restaurant to show Diana and the Bradshaws how to reach it, for neither of them had been there before. The drive was pleasant and fairly short, although a bit quiet for Diana, who hummed to herself to fill the silence. It was rather fun following Alex and having the pleasure of watching his head and profile as he drove unaware. At one traffic light, she saw him look in his rear-view mirror and waved her hand. He smiled, and she saw a lift of his hand in reply before the light changed.

She followed him into a parking lot, checking behind her to see if the Bradshaws had made the turn too. She barely had time to pull into the parking space beside Alex's when her door was opened and Alex's hand was guiding her out, locking the door behind her. They went into the small dark building with Owen and Grace following. She was pleased and not too surprised to see the luxurious interior of the restaurant. The lighting was muted and soft, and the colours of the décor were a pleasant mixture of browns, dark blues and golds. Alex turned to the others as they paused inside the door, and said, 'I made reservations for six-thirty, so we have about forty minutes. They have a bar downstairs and a dance floor, if you would like to watch the dancing for a while.'

Everybody agreed that that would be fun, so they headed down the wide staircase while Alex went to speak to the hostess at the front desk in the foyer. They had just found a small table near the corner in the crowded room with a clear view of the dance floor when Alex came up. He pulled a chair around to Diana's side and sat down. She pretended a nonchalance that she was nowhere near feeling as she sensed the strong leg so close to hers. Alex shifted closer to the small table and in doing so, came in contact with her leg. She glanced at him swiftly, almost absentmindedly, catching a wicked gleam in his very bright eyes that surprised her. 'That devil!' she thought. 'He's doing it on purpose.'

Just then, a cocktail waitress came up to the table and in the minor bustle of ordering drinks all around, Diana had turned to the waitress and in doing so, had shifted the barest fraction of an inch away from the contact with Alex.

Glancing at him quickly while he was talking to Owen on his right, she was discomfited to see a small slight smile that tugged at the corner of his mouth as if he couldn't help it. She was certain that he knew that she had moved away on purpose.

While Owen and Alex talked, Grace started to ask her about herself. She replied with monosyllables when questioned about her private life, but when Grace enquired about her past school life, Diana's face lit up and she answered eagerly. She had always loved school and the learning processes. They talked about the special bond that sometimes occurred between a teacher and a student. Grace then told her that she had been a teacher before she became too weak to handle the work load. 'I still keep in touch with some of my students,' Grace said, a thread of affection running through her voice as she recalled her special people.

A hand touched Diana's back and she jumped a little in surprise. Alex and Owen had gradually stopped talking and had listened to the women as they carried on their conversation. Now, Alex said with a smile, 'We have just enough time for one dance before we go upstairs, Diana. Shall we?' He stood and waited, ultimately giving her no choice.

She chuckled resignedly as she stood swiftly. Just one dance could do no harm, she thought. Nothing much could happen that she would not be able to control in one dance—except her own emotions. As Alex's arm curled around her waist, she felt a strange sensation in the pit of her abdomen, like a muscle contracting. He pulled her towards him and held her lightly as they began the first steps of the dance. Diana could feel the solid, tight muscles in Alex's shoulder where she rested her hand and again felt the impact of the sheer male strength of the man. She stared off unseeingly over his shoulder.

He held her away from him a little to see her expression a bit better. He smiled to see the unfocused look in her eyes. 'Penny for them,' he said softly.

'Hmm?' Her eyes turned to him. She had heard him well enough but she wanted a little time to collect her thoughts. She couldn't very well tell him that she was thinking about how good he felt against her so close. At that thought, her cheeks reddened, and Alex's grin widened.

'Your thoughts,' he supplied helpfully. 'Penny for them.' They swung around and around the dance floor. Diana shook her head.

'Do you mean to tell me that my intelligent, quick-thinking young right-hand "man" doesn't have a thought in her beautiful little head?' he taunted in derision. A smile broke out over Diana's face and it was like a flower opening into full bloom. He held his breath unconsciously as he watched her.

'No, it doesn't!' she informed him smartly. 'It means that your intelligent, quick-thinking, resourceful and witty right-hand person isn't going to tell you what thoughts she has in her wonderful and beautiful head!' His laughter rolled out over the heads of the other dancers, and heads turned to the tall attractive couple that was so obviously having a good time.

He asked her, 'What do you think of Owen's wife?'

She replied seriously, 'I think she's everything that her name implies. She does have an inherent grace in everything she does. She seems to be kindness in itself.'

'She is,' Alex said soberly, his voice deepening as he became serious too. 'Grace never complains, no matter how bad her asthma gets and no matter how tired and drained she becomes. It was quite a blow to her when she had to quit her job. She loved to teach so much.'

Diana moved one fingernail over the outline of the seam

on Alex's jacket absentmindedly as she listened. She said suddenly, 'I don't know what I would do if I couldn't work, if I was unable to be creative in the way that I want to be, if I were so—stifled.' She shivered. Days, she thought, endless, endless days marching on, never changing, never anything new or challenging, always the same monotonous thing. Depression. Frustration. Horror at the thought of being forced to such inactivity made her close her eyes.

Alex said gently, 'But Grace is so different from you, Diana. She told me once that she really doesn't mind staying home so much. It's the children that she misses. No, Grace is like a gentle summer rain that eases and soothes the mind on a quiet night. You, Diana, are like a prairie fire, swift-moving and intensely creative with constantly new and innovative ideas. You are colourful, and you need outside stimulus to stay colourful. I can admire Grace for her courage and strength in the way she handles her confinement, but you . . .' he touched her face with one gentle finger, '. . . you I would only pity, just like I would a wild bird in a cage.'

The music stopped and his hand fell away. Diana saw in her mind's eye a tiny wild thing beating itself frantically against the bars of a cage, bruising itself on the hard metal. Alex put a gentle hand under her elbow and guided her back to the table, talking harmless light conversation that needed no reply or response, until they reached the table where Owen and Grace sat.

Grace's eyes were bright. 'That looked like so much fun!' she said happily. 'It was almost as much fun as if I'd danced it myself!' Diana looked at her but could not reply.

Alex said smoothly, 'It was fun, Grace. Diana and I enjoyed it very much.' He looked around. 'Would you like to go on up now, or would you like another drink first?'

Everybody decided to go on up to dinner, so there was a

bustle for several minutes as they went up to the main floor for the meal. Diana ended up seated across from Alex, with Grace and Owen seated at opposite ends. The meal as things progressed was delightful and temptingly arranged, cooked to perfection. Talk flowed freely and lightly around the table. Alex and Owen had Grace and Diana laughing so hard that they were near to choking and had to beg the two men to kindly shut up until they had finished their meal. It was not until after dinner, when the coffee was being served, that Owen brought up something that had been in the back of Diana's mind all evening.

'So, Alex,' he stared into his coffee as he spoke, 'what do you think Payne will do now?'

Alex's face darkened and Diana saw a glimpse of the fury that he had tried so hard to keep suppressed. 'I don't know. He probably has his spies that have informed him that we have our Philadelphia foundry back in working condition. He's got to know that now he's got no chance. I have armed security guards at both foundries both day and night . . . you know, I could kill that bastard with my bare hands.' It was said lightly, almost conversationally, as if he had been discussing something so minor as the weather, but she looked down at Alex's big hands and thought of the strength in them and shivered. Remembering the frustrated anger she had felt herself over the past month or so, she had no doubt that she probably would want to help him murder Payne.

Tension was in the air and Diana made an effort to ease things a bit. 'So,' she said brightly, 'when do we take out a contract on him?' She put one elbow on the table and gestured with her hand. Everyone had looked at her in surprise. She continued, 'I know this fellow, he's really good with knives, a little expensive, but I'm sure we could work something out . . . ?' She looked around the table enquiringly. Grace had begun to laugh helplessly at the ridiculous look on Diana's face, and one eyelid dropped drolly as she turned to Alex. Owen chuckled and Alex after a moment was prodded into a smile, albeit a reluctant one. She was pleased to see the glow of rage in Alex's eyes fade away and he relaxed in his chair.

Diana looked pleased. Things had mellowed out nicely and Grace started to chatter about something else when some instinct made her look to Alex. He was watching her closely, one eyebrow cocked ever so slightly with a crooked smile twisting one side of his mouth. She lifted her eyebrows back at him and gave a tiny shrug as if to say, 'What else could I have done?' His shoulders shook faintly, and although his face was serious, she knew he was laughing. She turned her attention back to Grace.

They broke the dinner party up early since the next day was Friday, meaning work for Diana, Alex, and Owen. Everyone walked out to the parking lot together, still talking, reluctant to end what had been a pleasant evening. Grace said to Diana, 'You simply must come and see me some time soon, dear. I've enjoyed this evening so much.'

Diana promised warmly, 'I'd love to come and see you some time! What time is best for you? Weekends are the easiest for me.'

Grace looked pleased. 'Weekends are just fine, dear. Is Sunday afternoon too soon?'

Alex interrupted the conversation smoothly. 'Diana is going on a picnic with me on Sunday afternoon, so she won't be able to make it this week, Grace.'

Diana looked indignant. She cocked one eyebrow at Grace as she drawled, 'That is the first I've heard of it!' Grace started to laugh.

Alex grinned. 'Don't you remember promising me a few weeks ago that when all the Philadelphia mess was cleared away, we would go on a picnic?' he asked, a deceptively innocent look in his eyes. She distrusted that look immediately.

'We never set a date and you know it!' she retorted, putting one hand on her hip as she shook her head.

Grace put in: 'Next Sunday afternoon would be just fine with me, Diana. It doesn't have to be this week.'

'There,' he said, looking smug. 'See, now you have no choice in the matter.'

They said goodnight to the Bradshaws and Alex walked her to her car. She looked at him after unlocking her car door and there was an obstinate line to her jaw that he had never seen before.

She said softly, 'We'll see if I have a choice or not about that picnic.'

His eyebrows shot up. 'Oh, good!' he exclaimed. 'I just love a fight!' She opened her mouth to argue that she had not been fighting and he held up a hand. 'Not now, you'll spoil what's been a good evening. We'll talk about it tomorrow.'

'I don't want to talk about it tomorrow!' she protested. 'And I don't want to go on the picnic either, so we might as well just drop the whole—'

She couldn't talk any more, for he had clapped his hand over her mouth and was bundling her into her car swiftly. 'Tomorrow,' he promised in her ear before slamming the door on her ejaculations.

'I was not fighting!' she muttered just after the door slammed. She saw rather than heard Alex begin to laugh, and turned her head away. Now she really was determined not to go with him on that picnic!

CHAPTER FIVE

FRIDAY morning dawned with a cheerful glow and Diana, feeling very refreshed after an extra hour of sleep, met it with a smile. It was a wonderful lack of tension that made her feel so exuberant, forcing her to acknowledge with a rueful twist of the mouth how much Alex's absence and the consequent load of responsibility had affected her. Those weeks had been a veritable juggling act for both Diana and Alex. She juggled contracts and prospective buyers, and he had to deal with his workers, the repairs done at the Philadelphia foundry, the insurance companies, and the extra contract load that Diana threw at him as soon as she had the terms negotiated. Looking back, she wondered at the terrific strain that both she and Alex had worked under.

She had been so exhausted that she barely took the trouble to eat an evening meal before falling into bed. She wondered if he had felt the same way. He had apparently thrived on the extra work load. How had he felt in the evenings? Had he been too tired to want to eat, or had he taken the time to go out, and if he did go out, with whom did he go . . . ? She shied away from that thought like a cat jumping from hot bricks. She pretended with a fine show of disdain that she didn't want to know.

She dressed simply for the day, wearing a thin summer dress with tiny red and blue stripes running vertically on the white material. It was sleeveless and had a thin belt as its only accessory. Diana loved its comfortable fit. She checked the time quickly and hurried out of the apartment.

At the office, she spent a moment talking with Carrie before she went into the other room. She told Carrie about how enjoyable the evening had been with the Bradshaws and how much she had liked Grace. Then, bringing the discussion to a quick end, she hurried on into the inner room.

Alex was seated behind his desk when she entered and only briefly looked up. Handing her a pile of papers, he merely said, 'These came in this morning, see what you can do with them.' Diana took them silently and sat down to work.

They spent the whole morning working in almost complete silence, a companionable sort of quiet that was meshed with a thinking concentration. Diana immersed herself in the wording of the contract proposals and was genuinely surprised when Alex stretched hugely in his chair and said, 'Lunchtime, slave.'

She stuck her tongue out at him before asking pertly, 'How much time do I get to eat—fifteen minutes?'

He eyed her lazily. 'If you're lucky.' He ran his hand through his hair, a sure sign that he was concentrating on something hard. 'I wish I didn't have to go to that business lunch this afternoon. I wish I could send somebody in my place . . .' A gleam entered his eyes as his head swivelled towards her.

She immediately scrambled up, grabbed her handbag and headed for the door, chattering the whole while. 'I sure hope you find someone to send, of course you know I would if I could, but I have this luncheon date with a juicy, junky hamburger and I'd be really disappointed if I couldn't make the date . . .' She was out of the door and gone, still hearing the echo of Alex's shout of laughter as she escaped down the hall.

When she made it back after lunch, it was to find the office empty and dark. Turning on the lights, she sat down to work on the papers left over from the morning. Unable to keep her eyes away from the desk clock on Alex's desk, she kept track of the minute hand as it crept slowly around in a circle. When he finally walked into the office, the clock showed two o'clock.

'Hi,' she said simply, finishing a mark on her paper before she looked up. Alex had a curious expression on his face as he walked around his desk and sat down. 'What's happened?'

'Payne has raised his prices for steel up back to normal,' he replied, putting his elbows on the desk top and resting his fingers against his mouth. 'I guess that's one way to signal defeat.'

Diana mulled over Alex's words for a minute. She had a vague feeling of anticlimax, almost a feeling of disappointment. 'That's it?' She spread her hands as she asked incredulously. 'All that unbelievable tension, all those frantically busy working days, all that tension, and now it's all over?'

'Apparently,' he muttered almost to himself. 'I don't trust that son of a bitch, though. I'd sure like to know what he's thinking right now.'

'Is there anything else he could do?'

He looked at her with a sardonic curl of the lips. 'Nothing legally. That's what has me worried.'

'And you do have guards at both of the foundries, so there's nothing that he could do there,' Diana thought out loud. She glanced at him quickly and then away. 'Are you going to keep your lower prices?' She might as well have said, 'Are you going to break him?' Both she and Alex knew what she had meant. Diana looked down at her desk, dreading the reply. There was silence for a moment.

Alex had clenched his fingers tightly and his face seemed to be all angles as he said harshly, 'I don't know.' She understood his dilemma. Here was the man that Alex could have cheerfully killed in a good fight, but the dirtiest thing he could have done was give up. Now it would look like a coldblooded act of murder with Payne as the victim. There was no way that they could pin the guilt for the arson on Payne, for he had been too clever covering up that evidence. Mason Steel had kept quiet about the whole thing and Payne could easily plead ignorance of the whole thing. Alex was caught between the desire to break the man he hated, and the prudence of backing down. Diana felt suddenly very weary of the whole mess.

'Well, I think he deserves the worst you can give him,' she declared indignantly. 'I wouldn't blame you a bit if you did keep the lower prices, even for a little while, just for spite. 'I would!'

He smiled a little. 'You know just what to say at the right time, don't you? Well, I'll think about it over the weekend. Maybe I can divorce myself from my anger enough to make a decision then.'

They slowly got back to work, each involved with heavy thoughts. The afternoon passed as silently as the morning had. Diana, with one eye on the clock, started to quietly stack her finished work around five-thirty, and tidied her desk for the weekend. Putting the shoulder strap of her bag over one shoulder, she started to rise when Alex spoke without looking up.

'When would you like me to pick you up on Sunday?' She felt foolishly surprised. She'd rather hoped that he had forgotten about the picnic by now.

'I'm not going on Sunday,' she said stiffly. 'See you later.' And she headed for the door.

Alex was a very big man, but he could move with a surprisingly deceptive speed, and he was at the door before Diana was. 'What time?' he repeated softly, leaning against the door and effectively blocking her only exit.

She put her hands on her hips and glared at him. 'I tell you, I'm not going!'

He continued as if she hadn't spoken. 'I'm going to be visiting my parents on Sunday morning, so will one o'clock be all right with you?'

'I won't be home.'

'Where will you be?'

'Nowhere you know.'

'Give me directions.'

'Will you just give up?' she sighed.

'No, I won't! Why don't you want to go on the picnic?'

'You never asked!' Diana shouted at him. She whirled away from him, talking in angry tones. 'I will not be taken for granted, nor will I be railroaded into something as if my wishes don't matter! I mean more to me than that!'

Alex had raised his voice before, just like Diana, but now he seemed suddenly calmer. 'I thought I had asked last night.'

'You mean you tried to manipulate me last night in front of Grace and Owen so that I would say yes,' she accused him. 'Did it ever occur to you that a simple question might have got you a lot farther?'

He grinned charmingly, 'All right. Sit down over there. Go on, sit!' She reluctantly moved over to the easy chair that Alex pointed to, wondering what he was up to now. When she had sat down, he came over to the chair and knelt beside it. He took her hand and asked with a serious expression on his face, 'Diana, will you go on a picnic with me on Sunday, please, with whipped cream and nuts on top?'

She saw the twin devils dancing in his eyes and snatched her hand away. She tried to keep a straight face, but a bubble of laughter popped up and gurgled out before she could stop it. She looked away and then back again. He still had that same puppydog look on his face as he waited for her reply. She couldn't take it any more.

'All right!' she howled with laughter as she pushed him away from the chair. 'Just get that silly look off of your face, will you?'

Alex chuckled smugly, 'At least it gets me what I want.' He stood up lithely as he laughed. 'Shall I call you on Saturday to get directions to your apartment?'

'That will be fine,' she told him. 'I'll be home all evening. Do you have my number?'

'Yes, I still have it from when I called you from Pittsburgh,' he replied. 'I'll see you Sunday then?'

'Yes. Talk to you later.' She walked out of the door. As she passed Carrie, she gave a casual wave, secretly wondering how much Carrie had heard of their shouting. She shrugged. It didn't really matter.

As she drove home, she began to get very depressed. Alex had talked and charmed her into something that she knew that she should steer clear of. She thought about him on the way through the streets. His charm was a special kind of charm that wasn't fake or obscene. He was simply a considerate and thoughtful person, who happened to be quite handsome. No wonder all the ladies love him, Diana thought wryly. All those kisses on the side of the cheek and forehead, that was just him, appreciating someone else. I'm the one who's acting abnormally, she told herself. I'm the one who's reacting too strongly. If I take it casually, then it will stay casual. So easily said!

Diana was not used to physical contact. She had never had any warmth or affection shown to her and she didn't know how to take it. No loving parent had cuddled her or stroked her fondly, and in the area of physical affection, she was frozen. No wonder Alex threw her off her stride with his unaffected show of emotions and feelings! He was in a whole different league. It was a way of living that fascinated her and yet frightened her, for she didn't understand it. In Alex, she glimpsed a world alien to that which she had always known. While deep down in the secret places of her heart she acknowledged that her past experience of life had not been exactly satisfying or happy, she could not accept that his was better. And yet . . .

'Every time I get around him, I start losing all my resolve not to see him outside of business contact!' Diana hit the steering wheel with one hand as she muttered angrily.

She spent the weekend in an agony of indecisiveness. On the one hand she didn't want to go on the picnic, but on the other hand, she couldn't bring herself to call Alex and tell him. When he called she merely gave him directions how to get to her apartment. She realised that if she tried to back out, he would simply bulldoze her into coming. She would just have to see to it that she didn't go out with him again. She asked Alex if there was something she could bring for the picnic and he replied no. 'I'll bring everything we'll need,' he told her. 'How does baked chicken sound?'

'It sounds delicious,' she assured him.

'Good. See you tomorrow.' He rang off quickly, and Diana replaced the receiver thoughtfully. Now she really was committed to the picnic. She couldn't very well back out now.

She tidied up the apartment Sunday morning and then looked outside. It was a very bright and warm day for the beginning of September, but there was a definite change from the warmth of the summer. Now, when a stray cloud passed overhead, the wind blew chill. She changed into an old worn pair of jeans that hugged her figure, and a warm turtleneck sweater, cream coloured and woolly. The door bell rang and she went to answer it. It was Alex.

'Hi,' said Diana without any surprise. 'Would you like

to come in?' As she spoke, she eyed him approvingly. He had on a tight pair of dark jeans that flared slightly below the knee. A grey shirt was tucked in at the waist with a black cardigan sweater over it. His hair was windblown and there was a trace of red along his cheekbones.

'Not now, thanks, unless you're not ready,' he replied. She shook her head.

'All I have to do is lock the door,' she grinned, and ran back into the apartment to grab her key on the dresser. Shoving it in her pocket as she walked, she jiggled the doorknob to make sure the lock was latched, then slammed the door hard. As she turned towards the car, Alex tested the door to see if it locked.

'All set?'

'Yep,' she said. They went down the steps and Diana stopped short as she saw the black Porsche by the kerb. 'I didn't know you had two cars,' she remarked with surprise. His other car was a light blue Mercedes, very proper.

'This one is my fun car.' Alex patted the hood of the Porsche as he walked her to the passenger side and opened the door. 'The other one I use strictly for business.' There was a sun-roof on the car that was open.

Diana pointed to it and laughed, 'So that's why you look so ruffled up!'

He chuckled, 'I never can resist opening up the top when I drive. It really gets depressing when winter comes! Like it?' He climbed into the driver's seat.

'Like it!' she exclaimed. 'Just try to keep me from stealing it!' He laughed, and turned the key in the ignition. They took off from the kerb with the engine at a muted roar, and Diana knew that when she got home, she would have to tell Terry all about it.

Alex drove smoothly and well, heading for a main highway. Soon Diana was quite lost, not having lived in

New York very long, and all she knew was that they were headed roughly north.

'Where are we going?' She had to shout a little to be heard.

'To a little wood that I know of up here,' he named a place that was lost in the wind. 'Do you know it?'

'No. I don't know New York well yet.'

'You wouldn't know of this place unless you were taken there or unless you were a member of the club. It's very private.'

It's very exclusive, you mean, Diana thought, but kept quiet. She was just going to sit back and enjoy herself, and not make waves. After travelling for about half an hour, Alex signalled to turn right and turned down a small one-lane road. There were two signs on either side of the lane, saying, 'Private, No Trespassers. Poachers will be Prosecuted.'

They travelled down the lane for maybe a half a mile when Alex pulled over to the side of the road and told her to get out. He picked up a covered basket from the back of the car and preceded her down a little path. He acted as if he knew where he was going, so Diana shrugged her shoulders and followed. They walked in silence for a few minutes, listening to the call of birds overhead, when suddenly they came into a small clearing surrounded by tall trees and thick bushes with a little stream gurgling at the other end. There were rocks evenly spaced in the water, and she exclaimed with delight, 'Stepping stones!'

Alex set down the basket and grinned at her. 'That's a definite hint if ever I heard of one. Would you like to go exploring before we eat?'

She turned to him with her eyes shining, 'Oh, yes! I love to tramp in the woods.'

'Then tramping in the woods we will go,' he stated. 'Come on.' They left the picnic basket in the clearing and went over to the stream to look across. It seemed suddenly very wide to Diana and she glanced apprehensively at Alex. She was sure she would never make it. He caught the look and laughed. 'All right, little coward! I'll go first.' He grabbed her hand and started carefully across, steadying her when she got a little wobbly.

After they made it across the stream, they explored the woods and slopes for hours. They played hide-and-seek and Diana stumbled upon a small cove hidden by ferns and small bushes. She hid in the cave-like hollow that was situated near the bottom of a slope for the longest time, covering her mouth with one hand to stifle her chuckling as Alex came at first very near and then moved farther away and never finding her little hiding place. She listened to him call finally in exasperation when he gave up finding her, and instead of answering, she started to sneak out very quietly. She made it halfway up the slope when Alex spotted her and gave a shout. At that she shrieked and started to run pell-mell for the clearing. He roared and she almost fell from laughing so hard at the sounds of crashing behind her. She started to believe that she just might make it first to the clearing where the picnic basket was when something big behind her cannoned into her and tumbled her to the ground. Then she just dissolved into giggles at the sight of Alex with leaves sticking out of his hair. He had a hard time refraining from grinning.

'You think it's funny,' he gasped out in between breaths, 'that I damn near fall on my head on that crazy slope—where were you, anyway? I had no idea.'

'There's a little half-cave hidden with ferns,' she chuckled, explaining. 'If I'd just kept quiet, you wouldn't have found me in a million years!'

He snorted. 'I probably wouldn't have. I'd have given up long before then!'

She started to laugh again.

'You look really funny,' she choked out between sniggers. 'All those leaves sticking out of your hair!'

'You don't look a whole lot better,' he retorted. 'In case you hadn't noticed, you have some interesting dirt on the back seat of your pants from your precious hiding place.' He stood up and stretched out a hand to help her up. They laughed and talked as they walked the short way back to the clearing. Alex put his arm casually around her as they went. She made no objection; it seemed so right and natural a gesture.

Diana was surprised at the excellent basket of food that Alex had brought. There was baked chicken, a fruit salad with apples, oranges and walnuts, and boiled eggs and rolls. When she commented on the delicious fare, he smiled.

'I'm willing to bet you didn't think I had it in me,' he replied with a grin. He was leaning back on one arm while chewing enthusiastically on a leg of chicken.

'You're right, I really didn't. Mmm—this fruit salad is very good,' she murmured, licking the last bit of juice from her fork.

'I'll have to tell my mother how much you liked it.' Alex's voice was bland.

'Your mother? Was it her recipe that you used?' she asked. She caught a glimpse of his face as he fought to conceal an inner amusement and comprehension dawned. She said deliberately, 'Why don't you tell her how much I liked the rest of the meal while you're at it? Those homemade rolls were delicious.'

His eyes went to her face, but there was nothing there to tell him whether Diana suspected anything out of the ordinary. He lied without a flicker of expression to give him away, 'I'll have to check the recipe when I get home to see if it's one that she gave me.'

At that she snorted. He really had gone too far! She said

dryly, 'I meant you should tell her she did a terrific job fixing the meal. Not every mother would do that for her grown son.'

Alex laughed out loud. 'When did you guess that I didn't fix the meal?'

She grinned. 'I'm not really sure, but it wasn't anything you said, it was the expression on your face. You ought to be ashamed of yourself! You deliberately set out to deceive a poor unsuspecting girl like me!'

'"Poor, unsuspecting girl like you"?' he hooted in derision. 'Only a devious and conniving mind would have been able to guess that I didn't cook that meal—a mind that works like mine does. You would have done the same thing, my girl, given half the chance and with no culinary talents to speak of.' Alex wagged the chicken leg at her as he spoke.

They continued the light bantering conversation as they cleaned up the remains of the meal and packed what little was left over away in the picnic basket. Then, lying side by side, they watched the clouds in the sky and picked out various shapes that caught their imagination. Diana found a flying horse and a swan, and Alex found a grinning witch and a gnome, although no matter how hard she tried, she couldn't see how he had found a gnome in the oddly assorted lumps and bulges that he pointed to in an effort to show her where it was. Eventually she felt her eyelids grow heavy, and her answers to his comments grew shorter and shorter. Presently she fell asleep.

In sleep, Diana's face was changed subtly. Her face was relaxed as all faces are in sleep, and in the relaxation the lines of her cheeks appeared to be more vulnerable and young, the set of her mouth less tense and defensive. As Alex gazed down at her face, he was amazed at the difference the absence of tension made in her face. Awake, Diana always held herself in an unconsciously aloof manner; in repose her face always had a rather cold set to it, denying any familiarities, any unasked-for advances. She had a very light and easy charm in most conversation, but there was always a definite line that was almost physically drawn around her that clearly stated, 'Back off, no tress-passing allowed." Here, in sleep, for the first time Alex looked down at a totally defenceless Diana.

Flickering eyelids indicated that she was close to waking, and when she finally opened her eyes to look around, he was lying back in the grass with his hands linked behind his head as he contemplated the late afternoon sun. She noted the change in the sun's position with surprise. 'But I only just now shut my eyes,' she protested to him. He cocked an eyebrow and started to smile as she faltered, 'At least I thought I'd only just shut my eyes.' She watched him as he continued to look up at the sky. There was a thoughtful air about him; he seemed to be pondering some inner revelation or secret and he barely seemed aware of her existence. She sat up quietly and began to look at the sky too. She searched the whole expanse and had just started over when a voice spoke by her ear.

'What are you doing?' Diana jumped exaggeratedly and looked around with a good show of surprise.

'I'm just trying to see what's fascinating you so much,' she exclaimed with a false innocence. She peered up at the sky again. 'Nothing very interesting now, not even any funny cloud formations.'

He smiled, 'Did I seem far away? I'm sorry. No, you're right, there isn't really anything interesting up there. I was contemplating something else.' There was a silence for a few minutes. It was not an uncomfortable silence, but a companionable one, full of thoughts and easy sharing with no trace of emptiness. Alex asked suddenly, 'Would you tell me about yourself?'

Diana turned her head towards him in surprise. She hadn't been expecting this type of conversation. She said lightly, 'You didn't tell me this was going to be a deep sort of a thing. I don't have my notes prepared.' He didn't smile. She leaned back on one hand and began to recite in a parrot-like voice, 'Diana Carrington, born *1957*, educated at the Terrence Elementary School, Illinois, and later at the Farthington High School. She graduated with honours from the graduate programme at Rhydon University with her MBA and was promptly snatched up by the prestigious and innovative Mason Steel Co., where she is presently employed as the New York Operating Manager, working directly under the great Alexander Mason himself.'

He said impatiently, 'I know all that. I've read your application.'

'Then you know everything there is worth knowing,' she spoke easily.

'I want to know about your family, your parents. I want to know what kind of past you've had—has it been happy, has it been sad? What has made you the person you are?' he asked quietly, twirling a piece of grass between his thumb and forefinger. His expression gave away none of his feelings as he glanced at Diana's face with its hard expression and tense mouth, bearing no resemblance to the sleeping girl of a few minutes ago.

'When I told you there was nothing else of importance, I meant it.' She now spoke with no trace of lightness in her voice, but instead with a hard, uncaring tone that made Alex flinch inwardly.

'Surely your family life held some importance?' he continued, unknowingly causing a great ache in her chest as she took in his words. 'Where do they live?'

Diana's voice was expressionless, but her face was bleak. 'I don't know where I was born, and no one else does either. I was found outside a small church in a cardboard box with a note pinned to a ratty old blanket I was wrapped in that said, "Her name is Diana." My last name was given to me by the local authorities. I was no doubt some poor girl's bastard child,' her mouth twisted the words bitterly, 'someone too young and poor to raise me herself. I've lost count of the foster-homes I've lived in, and never bothered making friends because I moved too much. The elementary and high schools mentioned in my file are the ones from which I graduated. I've been to five—or was it six? I can never remember.'

Alex's face looked to be all angles as he listened to her monologue. His hand slowly crushed the slender blade of grass held in one hand and it dropped to the ground, mangled and forgotten. He said abruptly, 'But you've made good in spite of your past. Bad memories can be overcome.'

Diana shifted restlessly and looked at him sharply. She enquired, 'What bad memories?' His head snapped up and he met her gaze with narrowed eyes. She went on, hard and defiant, 'I didn't make good in spite of my past, I made it because of my past. I put myself through college and graduate school, no one else. The one thing I've always had is myself. I made me what I am today; I can always count on me to pull me through anything. I am my best provider. I clothe me and bathe my wounds and I put food on the table. As long as I have myself, I'll never go hungry. End of story.'

Alex said quietly, 'That's not all there is to living, Diana.'

She raised her eyebrows. 'That's all there is to my life. I'm not missing anything.'

'That's because you don't know anything else!' He paused and continued more carefully. 'There's a whole new dimension of emotion that you have yet to discover, a deeper and more—'

'An illusion,' she interrupted his sentence and he stared at her, incredulous at her statement. 'It's all an illusion, Alex. None of it is real or reliable. Rely on yourself only; in the end it's all you'll have. No—don't bother.' It was all said harshly as she forestalled his attempt to speak. 'Whatever you're going to say, I don't want to hear it. When I said that all I ever had was myself, I wasn't complaining. That's all I've ever needed.'

There was a quietness, a stillness that had nothing to do with the sounds of nature that surrounded them. Neither Alex nor Diana looked at each other. Then she said softly, 'It's been fun. I think it's time we headed back, though.'

'To reality?' Alex was sarcastic, his face a mask.

'Of course.'

He was still for a moment before he finally nodded. They packed the things in the car and drove back. The trip was silent. Alex was intent on his driving, his eyebrows lowered in a frown and his mouth in a straight line. Diana was aloof, thinking her own thoughts and wearing her pride like an invisible mantle, sheltering herself from the outside world. The car pulled up to the kerb outside her apartment and she turned to thank him, but he was opening his door.

'I'm seeing you in,' he said tersely.

She shook her head. 'There's no need . . .' she began, but he interrupted her.

'I know you don't need it,' the sarcasm was still evident in Alex's voice and Diana stared at him. She had never heard that particular bitter note from him before. 'But I never take someone home without seeing her inside, if you don't mind.'

She shrugged and slid out of the car too. As they walked up the sidewalk, still with that charged silence from the trip home, she was aware of a violent emotion that emanated from Alex's person. She was confused by it and she couldn't identify with it. She walked warily with this unknown person. At the door, she reached in her pocket for her front door key, and inserted it into the lock. Alex turned the knob and pushed the door open, propelling her in with one hand at her back as he followed quickly. She began to protest in anger since she had had no intention of inviting him in, but he told her to shut up. They faced each other in the shadowed hallway.

After staring down at Diana's face and seeing another, more vulnerable face in his mind, he began to talk in a low voice. 'I believe you when you say you've never needed anyone before in your life. I think you're right to count on yourself to pull you through a crisis. But there is a better way of life than that, Diana. You did fine when you had to survive, but that's all you know how to do, survive. I've seen too many examples of another way of life, a better and deeper . . .'

'We had a pleasant day, didn't we?' she interrupted. He fell silent as she continued, walking away. 'I think you'd better leave it at that.' She didn't want to hear what Alex had to say.

'Damn you, don't walk away from me!' His hand shot out and pulled her roughly around to him as he spoke. She jerked her arm away and stepped back.

'I'll do what I please in my own time, Mr Mason!' she hissed, furious at his rough handling.

Goaded, he grabbed her by the shoulder and started to shake her. He exclaimed, 'My God, are you an iceberg, all frozen and hard—'

'I don't have to hear this!' she cried out, pushing him as hard as she could in an effort to break his hold. She felt nothing like the iceberg Alex had called her. Something deep in her chest was licking at her very core of being like tiny tongues of flame. It hurt incredibly. 'Who in hell are you to be talking to me this way? I don't need anybody's criticism, I'm not ashamed of what or who I am!' Never before had Diana felt so threatened by another person; now she was frightened, and fear made her lash out. 'You have no right to speak like this to me, you just can't take someone living differently from you—'

He let her go suddenly and she very nearly fell. 'What the hell are you implying?' he asked through his teeth. She could feel his rage burning her.

She suddenly wished she hadn't said anything. 'Nothing.' She tried to pass off her remark with a downward jerk of her hand.

'No,' he softly spoke. 'You meant something by what you said, and you were going to say more. What was it? I mean to know!' He was really furious.

'I was referring to your social life,' she said suddenly, letting it all out, sick and tired of the whole nasty scene. She continued coldly, 'From what I've heard, you lead quite a different life from my own quiet one. What am I, a challenge or something? A possible conquest for your male ego?'

He stiffened, sucking in his breath audibly, letting it out as he spoke. 'No, I don't consider an emotional cripple a possible conquest. That is you, isn't it? You don't know how to feel.'

'What's it to you?' she shouted suddenly, moving around the dark room like a hunted animal. She wanted to beat her fists against his chest to hurt him as much as he was hurting her. 'I'm doing just fine on my own, I don't need advice from you or anybody else! I'm a perfectly healthy, normal woman and I can look after myself—'

'You can feed yourself, protect yourself, and never have to care for anybody else—what kind of existence is that? You never ache, or cry or bleed for anybody else—God, I pity you!' He was a silhouette, a dark shape in the deepening dusk as he stabbed the air in front of him with one forefinger while his voice ripped her into shreds.

Diana stood very still and straight as she fought a war with her own emotions, emotions that Alex's attack evoked. Then she said one thing, devoid of all feeling or anger. 'Get out.'

Alex's whole body was held tensely. She could feel it from where she was standing. Then he let out an explosive sigh and the taut lines of his body relaxed. 'Diana, we've said so much in anger, I'd like to—'

'What anger?' she interrupted. She had to get him out of there. Moving to the wall where the light switch was, she flicked it and the room was set into a much sharper relief as the mellow lighting flooded everything with a yellow tinge. It was a mistake, for now she could see his face and read his expressions. 'No,' she continued quietly, looking very much in control (she had to get him out), 'I feel no anger now, although you're right, we have said too much. I think we should leave it for tomorrow, and settle anything we feel we need to when we've got some rest.' Her face was very calm now, and very cool (Get him out of here, please God, before I break apart).

'I think we should settle it now!' he snapped harshly, moving with a violence akin to that of a savage animal. She sucked in her breath at the anger she had caused in him with her dismissing words.

'Then you can talk to an empty room,' she snapped back coldly. She was feeling really desperate now, and her hands were shaking. She had to get rid of him. 'I'm going to bed. Lock up when you leave, will you?' She started for the room down the hall. It seemed like a haven to her now. She didn't look back as she called over her shoulder. She could hear his footsteps as he started to follow her. 'Don't bother trying to come in my room, Alex. If you do, I'll simply scream, and Terry and Brenda, who happen to feel very protective about me, will be up here in a moment. You wouldn't want that kind of a hassle, would you?' She had reached her room and she walked in with a fine show of confidence. 'Goodnight, Alex.' She shut the door, then moved over to the bed and sank down into it, covering her face with her shaking hands. She could hear no sound coming from the other room. She waited for a little while, how long she had no idea. Then she moved over to the window and looked out.

A sleek black car was pulling away from the kerb.

Diana collapsed on her bed and shook all over. When she finally roused herself, it was only to set the alarm for the next morning. She didn't even bother to undress, but merely crawled under the top cover after turning out the light.

CHAPTER SIX

THE elevator doors opened and Jerry looked out with a big grin when he saw who was about to enter the elevator. Then the grin slowly faded as he took in the appearance of the other person.

'Gee, Miss Carrington,' Jerry exclaimed, 'you look kinda tired today!'

Diana smiled faintly at the note of concern in Jerry's voice. 'I feel kinda tired,' she said with a sigh. There were dark bruise-like circles under her eyes and her cheekbones stood out sharply. The only colour she had on her face was the colour that she had applied with make-up. The night had been bad.

'Maybe you should go home and go to bed,' he suggested. She chuckled a little and he felt relieved. She looked better when she laughed. Not normal, but better.

'I just got out of bed, Jerry,' she grinned. 'I wouldn't be able to sleep if I wanted to.'

'Did you have a hard weekend?' Jerry asked sympathetically.

'No.' Diana shook her head. 'I just can't seem to unwind even though Mr Mason is here to take some of the work load again.'

He nodded sagely. Everybody had been aware of the hard hours that Diana had put in when Mr Mason was gone. 'It'll take you a while to get to normal again, I reckon.'

The elevator doors opened and he stepped back. 'Have a good day, Jerry,' Diana stepped off the elevator as she spoke.

'You too, Miss Carrington. 'Bye!'

The day went about as badly as she had expected, but for a different reason from what she had expected. When she went into the office, she was greeted by a very polite Alex who made no reference to last night at all. Diana was surprised and a little let down, for she had been keyed up all morning for a confrontation that never came.

Alex looked a little better than she did, but he still had an odd set to his face which made it seem older, more harsh. Whenever he talked to Diana, it was with a chill formality that began to grate on her nerves. With Carrie and Owen and everyone else, he was the same warm and joking Alex that she had known from before their argument, but his politeness with her never changed. She went home at the end of the day more exhausted than if they had spent the whole day fighting.

The next few days were the same way, only a little bit worse, because under the chill politeness that Diana and Alex showed one another, they began to snap as the tension started to build. Carrie noticed the change, and although she made no comment, Diana knew that occasionally Carrie's worried eyes followed her around the office.

One afternoon Diana watched Alex with Owen and the way his face was alight with laughter over something Owen had said. She was hesitant to interrupt, but needing Alex's signature on something, she had broken in quietly. She had felt such an acute pain when she had seen the way a mask had slid over Alex's face when he had turned towards her, leaving—nothing. She wondered that she did not start to cry then and there, but she had pretty well maintained her composure, although her hands had trembled as they accepted the signed papers. Owen's farewell that day was very kind.

On Wednesday, as she was preparing to go home, she

was surprised to turn and see Alex at her elbow. He stood looking down at her frowningly until she finally said with a biting edge of anger, 'What do you want?'

His face was very hard when he heard her tone, but he didn't comment. Instead he asked, 'Do you have anything planned for tomorrow night?'

Surprised, she answered without thinking, 'Nothing much, why?'

'There's a business dinner I would like you to attend tomorrow night. We have a new client who needs to be wooed and won, and he's bringing his wife. You're the logical choice to come and make numbers even.' He stood waiting for an answer as she thought rapidly, replanning her evening schedule. She finally nodded.

'I think I can make it,' she said, and he nodded.

'Good.'

The next day went very much the same as the previous days had gone. Diana was very tired of the constant tension she felt whenever Alex was around. She was glad of the chance to go home early on the pretext of getting ready for the dinner that night. It was getting cool in the evenings, so she happily took out her dark red dress with a black pair of high-heeled shoes to wear with it. She set her hair with hot curlers and brushed it to hang free except for one side that was pulled back with a gold comb. She then added an extra touch of red lipstick and reshadowed her eyes. With a look at the clock, she swung a beige coat on to her shoulders and left her apartment.

She was to meet Alex at the office parking lot and then Alex was going to drive to the little restaurant where they had eaten with the Bradshaws before. She was glad the trip would be fairly short from the office to the restaurant. She didn't know how she would be able to put up with Alex's coldness all evening as it was.

He was in the parking lot when she pulled in. He

opened the door of her car and stood beside it as she locked the door. Then he held open the passenger door for her as she climbed in.

She was relieved when Alex, after starting the engine and pulling out of the lot, began to tell her about the prospective client that she was to meet tonight. His voice was cool and professional and Diana found it easy to relax and pay attention. Mr Valsing and his wife were from southern California and were on a business-cum-pleasure trip for several weeks in New York. Diana understood. Mr Valsing was here on business and Mrs Valsing was here for pleasure. Brent Valsing was a rabbit of a man, Alex told her with a tinge of amusement in his voice. Diana couldn't wait to see what Vanessa Valsing was like. She had an idea already.

When Alex performed the introductions between the Valsings and Diana, she had to keep a firm hold on her sense of humour. She had been right. Vanessa Valsing was a slightly plump woman who was the very last word in lacquered perfection. Every dyed hair was in perfect place, and her eyelashes were so long (good God, they had to be false!) that they batted her thinly pencilled eyebrows. Her long, long nails were painted a very bright red, and jewels glittered at her throat, arms and fingers. There was a slight sag to her chin and wrinkles radiated in a crows-feet pattern from her eyes.

Brent Valsing was only slightly shorter than Diana, but with his rather too thin shoulders and his slightly thickening middle, he seemed even shorter. His hair was thinning on top, and although he had rather nice eyes, the whole effect was spoiled by his moist mouth and the peculiar way he had of forming his words. Diana's eyes kept returning again and again to his mouth in a horrified fascination whenever he spoke. It was as if, she thought with an inward chuckle, his two lips were made of rubber and he had a particularly trying time whenever he wanted to form a word. She tried to imagine him kissing, and the very thought made her shudder.

The one thing she was unprepared for was when Alex put a casual arm around her shoulders as they headed down the stairs to the dance floor. Nor did she miss the sudden narrowing of Vanessa Valsing's cat-bright eyes as she took in the movement. When they all sat down to one of the little round tables by the dance floor, Diana was never sure afterwards how Vanessa contrived to sit in between Diana and Alex and across from her husband. Diana mentally shrugged her shoulders and sat down to make the best of the situation. After a few minutes of uttering bright nothings around the table, Vanessa gave a little wriggle of her shoulders that did funny things to her bosom and declared in a little-girl voice, 'Alex dear, you really must dance one dance with me. I'll never ever forgive you if you don't!' And so, with a smile, Alex led Vanessa off on to the dance floor.

Brent turned to Diana with a smile that was meant to be charming, but instead was merely wet. Diana, inwardly cringing, pulled her lips into a response that she could only hope did not appear as fakey as it felt. As they circled the dance floor, she listened with one ear to Brent's dull and steady explanation of how his family had inherited wealth for generation after generation, making them the very best of families to marry into. '. . . And of course Vanessa comes from the Strattons from Kentucky,' he imparted gravely. Diana nodded with a suitable look on her face as she wondered just who in hell were the Strattons from Kentucky. As they circled around, she happened for just an instant to face Alex as they both looked over the shoulders of their respective partners. Vanessa was making an extravagant gesture which Diana mimicked with her hand that rested on Brent's shoulder, and Alex's face flooded with laughter. Then they were gone and Diana was left with only Brent and her own devices.

After the first dance, Diana and Brent were heading back to the table when Alex and Vanessa appeared beside them. Alex said smoothly, 'Shall we go on up to the table?'

Vanessa pouted prettily, 'Oh, I would like just one more dance, Alex. Wouldn't you?' She was looking up at Alex as she talked, but he was looking at Diana.

'I really should dance one dance with my assistant, don't you think?' He was suave as he sidestepped Vanessa's blatant invitation. 'How rude of me if I didn't.' A strong arm reached out and encircled her waist and they were swinging away from the Valsings before she knew it.

'You, madam, nearly got me into trouble a few minutes ago,' Alex murmured into her ear as they moved away. She leaned back against his arm to look at his face in surprise.

'What did I do?' she asked. He had his head bent close to hers and she could smell the clean scent of his aftershave. She had the strangest urge to put her face closer to his and nuzzle his chin.

'Dear Vanessa wanted to know just what I found so funny about diamonds—which was what she'd been talking about when you so comically did your thing—and I had to do a neat bit of improvising to explain,' Alex grinned as he spoke. Lights gleamed in his chestnut hair and his vivid eyes as they whirled around and around. Diana didn't look at anything else, trusting instead to Alex's guidance as she stared up into his face.

'I'm sure you handled things quite well,' she murmured. 'I've heard you always handle the ladies well.'

He laughed and tightened his arm around her waist. 'You're in trouble for that statement!'

All too soon the dance ended and Alex led the way back

to the table, leaving her to come down to earth by herself. She slowly became realistic; magic such as that of the dance and of the picnic many days ago was like a fantasy that had no part of the world as she knew it. Interludes were nice now and then, but she mustn't allow them to cloud her perspective. She felt a great anger towards herself for her apparently illogical reactions to Alex. Now, in the midst of a tremendous rift between the two of them, she was attracted to him as never before. It was a contradiction and an affront to all she considered strong and unwavering in herself.

The dinner was long and very tiring for Diana. She quickly grew weary of the Valsings and their own brand of mediocrity. Vanessa had an infuriating way of either ignoring her completely or making some comment to her that was light enough on the surface, but had a dig underneath. She had a great contempt for those sort of catty remarks, and Vanessa found that most of her maliciousness bounced off a completely blank face.

Brent tended to chew his food like he talked, and all through the meal, Diana tried to look everywhere but at him, which at times was a little difficult when he directly addressed her or she him. It helped that she sat across from Alex, so for the better part of the meal she looked at him in desperation.

It was over coffee and dessert when business was finally brought into the conversation. Brent finished his pie with a final shovel towards his mouth and sat back, sighing. 'Good meal,' he grunted. 'But I suppose it's time to get down to what we really came to discuss.' Vanessa, unnoticed by anyone, settled back in her own seat with a smile. 'Alex, I have just one question that I'd like to get answered: Why did you raise your prices again this week when you could have put Payne out of business?'

Diana began to fiddle with her napkin without looking

at anybody. Alex had made his decision at the beginning
of the week, and as far as she knew, everybody at the office
had carefully steered clear of any mention of the subject.
She wondered what Alex was going to say.

His answer was simple and unrevealing. All he said
was, 'I never set out to destroy anybody's business and I
won't start now. Payne has got to make it or go under on
his own steam. I don't want anything to do with him.' And
that, she judged by Alex's closed expression, would be all
that was said about *that*. The two men went on to discuss
various aspects of a possible contract deal which she had
the good sense to stay out of. Vanessa, however, was a
different matter. If she did not like a certain wording or a
certain promise, she said so in a very pretty voice until it
became apparent that Brent was going to do anything
Vanessa said he should do. Diana got a clearer picture of
the Valsing household as the discussion went on. Brent
was in New York to conduct business and Vanessa was
here to see that he did it right. She sat back in her chair
and waited silently for the end of the evening.

It came fairly quickly. As soon as Alex realised what
was going on, and that the conclusion of the deal de-
pended on the approval of a rather capricious woman, he
politely but firmly put an end to the discussion. 'My staff
will put together a contract proposal by tomorrow afternoon so that you'll have something in writing to study,' he
said with remarkable patience. He ostentatiously looked
at his watch. 'And now, I'm afraid, we're going to have to
leave. I still have work to do tonight and I'll have to start it
soon if I'm to be done by midnight.' After many protests
and explanations, he stood up and motioned to Diana that
they had to leave. The farewells were pleasant enough,
and the walk out of the restaurant was even more
pleasant. She settled back in the seat of the car with a huge
sigh of relief.

He asked sympathetically, 'Was the evening as bad as all that?'

Shaking her head, she said with a chuckle, 'No, it would have been worse if the evening had been longer.'

He laughingly agreed. 'The worst part had to be the dancing!' he exclaimed. 'If Vanessa had put on any more perfume, I think I'd have suffocated!'

'And Brent with his rubber lips,' she began to giggle again as she pictured in her mind his face. 'And who in the world are the Strattons from Kentucky?'

Alex shook his head and his shoulders shook with mirth, 'I don't know! Some aristocratic horse nuts, I guess!'

'Oh, Alex dear, you must dance one more dance with me, or I'll be terribly hurt, simply terribly!' she trebled in a falsetto mimicry of Vanessa's particular brand of charm. Alex had tears in his eyes from laughing so hard.

The drive back to the Mason parking lot where Diana's car was parked was accomplished in an amazingly short time. She looked around as Alex pulled up the car beside hers and thought, 'It's been too short. Tomorrow we go back to all the strains and tensions that were there before tonight, and it will be as if this pleasant comradeship had never been.' Tomorrow. She turned her head to look at him as he switched off the car.

He felt it too, and when he spoke there was a tone of formality in his voice that seemed to put a barrier between them. 'I never thanked you for rearranging your schedule so that you could come tonight,' he told her quietly. 'You helped carry things beautifully during the evening.'

Diana gave a little shrug and spoke diffidently. 'I rather thought I was the cause of tension tonight, for some reason. Vanessa didn't appear to—well, she probably would have been happier—that is, I'm sure you could have handled things very well on your own.'

He looked at the steering wheel in front of him. 'She wasn't exactly affectionate towards you tonight, was she?'

She gave a little laugh. 'No, I don't think affectionate was quite the word for how she felt towards me!'

'Envy would be more like it, wouldn't it?' Alex still didn't look at her.

She frowned. 'I don't quite follow you.' Jealousy would have been the word that she would have chosen. An ill-founded, irrational jealousy a married woman had no right to feel, just because an available and attractive male showed a little attention to someone else beside her. Diana pictured the narrow, cat eyes again when Alex put his arm across her shoulders.

'I think that it's very understandable,' he continued. 'Here you have a very insecure woman who's trying desperately to hold on to what good looks she has, while she knows deep down that whatever attractiveness she had any claim to is rapidly fading into plump middle age. She looks at you, with your tall slimness and beautifully proportioned body, and your vibrant colouring, and feels drab. Even her husband pays attention to you. No wonder she feels the need to alternately strike out at you, who threatens her, or woo every man in reach—who happened to be me. She was trying to establish her own worth.'

'I never thought of it like that,' Diana murmured, taken aback. Someone actually feeling threatened by her!

'No,' he agreed with a strange tightness to his voice. 'No, you wouldn't, would you? You only think of yourself in terms of logic and reason. You never leave any room for the irrational or the emotional. You have it all figured out.'

'I never said that!' She swung her head as she snapped.

'You wouldn't know what it would be like to need others approval or acceptance,' he continued relentlessly. There was a deep glow of what looked like anger in his eyes and she wondered why in the world he would be angry with her. 'You don't understand people like Vanessa who want to be attractive to others.'

'Will you just shut up!' Diana hissed, her lips tight across her teeth. 'What reason do you have for talking to me like this? I didn't ask for it!'

'That's right. You don't need other people, their criticism or caring. You're a totally self-sufficient entity, aren't you? Just like a machine, Diana.' His voice had risen and she found herself shouting back.

'And don't you forget it!' she yelled. They glared at each other for a moment. Diana straightened her shoulders and withdrew perceptibly. She spoke and her voice was very cold. 'I don't need this conversation, I don't need other people, and I certainly don't need you.' She fumbled for the door latch, her face turned away from him.

Suddenly she was jerked back around to face him and she stared up into his white face and glowing eyes. Good lord, is he in a rage, she thought dazedly to herself, and then he was speaking. '. . . never need anybody, do you? I just wonder if you know how to want somebody.' He started to lower his head towards hers and she felt a sudden panic when she realised his intention. She pushed him as hard as she could with both hands against his shoulders, but it was like pushing a granite wall as she felt the latent strength of his body. 'My God,' he breathed, 'I bet you've never even been kissed!' He held her head firmly with one hand behind it, and then his mouth was on hers. She was very shocked at the primitive feelings that Alex aroused in her, feelings she had never experienced before. She had a dazed impression of a hard pressure on her lips that slowly started to ease and soften, and a large looming bulk of strength that was huge before her, and as Alex's arms slid to hold her, around her. She didn't even try to think, for she was too busy experiencing the fascinating realm of feeling when Alex jerked back. His breathing was harsh as he stared down into her widened eyes and at her tumbled hair. Then he set her roughly back on the seat and snapped hardly, 'That's what it's like to want somebody!'

She sat a moment, holding herself very still. Then without a word, she quietly opened her car door and got out. There was really nothing to say. Alex started his car, not waiting to see if she got in her car safely, backing away as soon as she had closed the passenger door.

When she was at home and in bed, Alex's words kept tumbling over and over again in her mind, like a broken record. Wanting? There was no question of wanting him. She had wanted him since the first time she looked at the length of his body. She had just been ignorant of what to name it. As she lay in bed, she could again feel the pressure on her lips, and the impression of hard arms around her body. It was almost as if he was here, in the room, and all she had to do was to reach out across the pillow ... damn! She cursed at her own imagination. Then, with a violent shudder, she put a hard discipline on her thoughts. She might want him, but she sure as hell did not need him. Sleep came fitfully for Diana that night.

The next morning when she reached the office, she had barely stepped inside the door when Alex snapped at her. Outraged and furious, she retaliated. All morning long they were like two animals, continually snapping and snarling. This time, even Carrie was drawn into the mood when Alex nearly reduced her to tears over a mistake she had made over the phone to a client.

When Carrie had left the room, Diana rounded on him. 'There was no good reason for you to upset her so much over a simple mistake!' she spat at him angrily. He stared back at her with a stony expression on his face.

'I don't see that it's any of your business what I do,' he

spoke, emphasising each word. There was a tautness in
the way he held himself, an anger that was controlled in
every movement.

'I don't give a damn what you do,' she retorted, her eyes
flashing. 'But you know and I know that your temper had
nothing to do with Carrie herself, but it was an outlet for
some stupid sort of anger you're feeling towards me. Well,
don't take it out on other people, because it's none of their
business! If you can't take it out on me then keep it to
yourself!' She turned away from him, her face hard.

Suddenly her shoulders were grabbed in a bruising grip
and she found herself twirled around and shaken hard.
She held herself rigid, refusing to relax or give way under
the hardness of Alex's hands. He stopped as quickly as he
started and they stared at each other for a moment. He
thrust her away from himself and turned to pace the room
in jerky movements, unlike his usual co-ordinated grace.

Diana also moved unsteadily as she groped for her
chair, unable to see through eyes blinded with tears. Her
shoulders were throbbing where Alex had gripped them
so hard, but she hardly noticed the pain aside from a
fleeting thought of what marks she might find tomorrow.
A drop of wetness spilled over and on to her hands as she
gripped them together on her desk top. She didn't pay any
attention.

'Dear God!' He spoke and she visibly jumped as she
took in his unexpected nearness. She hadn't been aware of
his approach. He stood looking at her, his face very pale
and his eyes darkly shadowed. His hands were clenched to
his sides and the knuckles showed white against the dark
hairs. He moved and she was being held very gently
against his chest with his face in her hair. 'Diana, I'm
sorry. Never in my whole life have I done that to someone.
I didn't mean it, I didn't mean to—I'm sorry. I'm sorry.'
He stroked her hair over and over as he crooned the

words. She moved her face for a moment, hiding in his broad, comforting shoulder. It was hard to comprehend just what she was feeling; pain of this sort was an entirely new experience. She wondered how she had ever existed without experiencing it before. Something inside her stiffened and she moved away from Alex sharply. She stared at him without expression, her eyes bitter and stony; she hated him for what he made her feel.

He drew his breath in sharply at what he read in her face and began to speak, but she cut him off. 'Don't be sorry, Alex.' She almost didn't recognise her own voice, it sounded so strange. Her lips moved in an imitation of a smile. 'I can take anything you dish out. It doesn't matter to me.' She watched his face go blank as he took in her words, his eyes focused on her yet unseeing. She looked away and at her desk. 'If you don't mind, I'll get back to work. After all, it's what I'm being paid for.'

She pretended to concentrate on her opened briefcase in front of her when she sat down, and she didn't look up when Alex left the room without explanation.

The rest of the day was spent in near silence. Alex was very remote, almost as if he didn't recognise the presence of someone else in the room. Diana rarely looked up from her desk in an effort to totally immerse herself in what she was working on, but it didn't work. She made more mistakes than she had ever made before in her life, and by the end of the afternoon was almost crying with frustration. She left the office without saying goodbye and hurried home to go straight to bed. The day had exhausted her so much that she fell immediately into a deep sleep and didn't stir all night. In the morning, when she finally opened her eyes, she had the feeling of being drugged from too much sleep, and she was horrified to find out how late in the day it was. She jumped out of bed quickly. Even though it was Saturday, she still had a lot to do, for tomorrow she had promised to go and see Grace Bradshaw. There was a heavy load of work waiting for her: the apartment needed cleaning and groceries had to be bought. Diana threw herself into the day's chores with something akin to desperation and did not stop until late in the evening when she was forced to stop from sheer exhaustion. Again, her night's sleep was deep to the point of being dreamless and the morning found her listless and tired. She did not attempt to get dressed until it was time to go in the afternoon, spending the morning in an aimless fashion as she drank coffee and lazed over the Sunday paper.

Grace was happy to see her; Diana watched her face light up with pleasure when she answered the front door. Eagerly talking, Grace led her into a comfortable sitting room and took her light coat to hang up in the hall closet. Diana chose one of the big armchairs near a fireplace when she saw a tea set near one with fresh pastries on a tray.

Grace came back almost immediately, her face crinkled into a broad smile. 'Oh, good,' she exclaimed, 'You've made yourself comfortable. Now we can sit and have a really good talk. Aren't these pastries nice? Here, have one. Mrs Cummings is a very good cook, and we're lucky to have her. How are you, my dear? You look so tired.'

'I've slept too much this weekend,' she smiled. 'That's as bad as not sleeping enough.'

Grace laughed. 'Isn't it, though? But tell me, how was the picnic last Sunday? Did you and Alex have a good time?' Grace was alarmed to see an expressionless mask drop over Diana's face before she replied. Owen was telling things accurately when he had said that there had been an unusual amount of tension at the office lately, and Grace made a sudden shrewd guess as to why.

Diana said carefully, 'We had lovely weather that day

and Mrs Mason packed a delicious lunch for us. It couldn't have been any nicer.'

Grace paused, then asked diffidently, 'So you had a nice time on Sunday?'

'The picnic was lovely,' Diana said truthfully, for indeed it had been, except for the end.

Grace was reluctant to leave it at that, but she was in the end very tactful. Instead she asked Diana how she found her work and if she was finding everything within her ability to understand and to cope. Diana relaxed a little and was able to respond with a more natural reply. They were able to talk about most things without any uncomfortable snags and the time passed very pleasantly, until car doors were heard slamming outside and Grace stood up. 'That must be Owen!' she exclaimed as she hurried to the front door. 'He'd met Alex at the office to go over a few problems and was supposed to be back about a half hour ago.'

Diana idly listened to the voices coming from the front door and suddenly sat up straight. A deep voice was talking back to Grace, the words unintelligible, but the tone unmistakable. Alex had come back with Owen. She made a deliberate attempt to relax and settle back in her chair, only to look down at her hands and start with surprise at her clenched fists. She loosened them as footsteps sounded near in the hall.

Alex was the first in the room, with Grace and Owen following. He slowed abruptly when he saw Diana in the armchair, and his nostrils flared as his head drew back. Then everything was almost too normal with Alex being too polite, and Diana, knowing it all to be a front, almost didn't bother to respond. It really was a bit ridiculous, she thought, looking around. Everybody knew something was wrong, but everybody was trying their very best not to show that they knew it. She met Alex's gaze, and they stared at one another for a long moment. She quickly stood up. 'Grace, I really must be going,' she said with a smile. 'The afternoon is almost gone and I hardly know where it went! Thank you for a lovely talk, and I promise to come again soon.' She turned to Alex and if her eyes didn't quite meet his, nobody else could tell. 'I'll see you tomorrow, Alex.'

His tone was sarcastic. 'So long, Diana.' He made no attempt to move his long legs and she had to step over them on the way to the doorway.

'Oh, Diana,' Grace called, 'don't go! You need your coat.'

Alex was on his feet very quickly. 'Sit down, Grace, I'll get it for her. Is it in the front closet?' Diana turned reluctantly; she didn't want to be alone with Alex, even for a few minutes in the hall. Alex brushed ahead of her and out to the hall and she followed, feet dragging.

He opened the closet door and looked in it briefly. Pulling out a coat, he held it up. 'Yours?'

She nodded. 'Yes.' Alex held open the coat and she turned to put her arms through the sleeves. There was a brief moment when his hands rested lightly on her shoulders, and then he was stepping back from her. She turned to thank him and her words faltered at the cold blaze in his eyes. He shook his head sharply when she had begun to speak.

'Don't bother,' he said abruptly. 'We both know that you didn't need the help.'

Diana closed her eyes. 'Dammit, why don't you just leave me alone?' she whispered. 'Why can't you just shut up and leave me alone?'

He stared at her a minute, a dark flush on the line of his cheekbone. He took her face in his two hands. 'I can't,' he hissed between his clenched teeth. 'The waste of any human being is a terrible thing to see.'

'But then, to listen to you, I'm not human, am I?' she said cynically. His hands dropped; he stepped away.

'That's right. You're not human.' He moved to the door. 'I have to move my car so you can pull out. No sense in wasting time—come on.'

Diana followed him out of the house, stumbling over the doorstep a little as his words echoed in her mind. 'No sense in wasting time.' He regarded her as a waste of time. It doesn't matter, she told herself. Nobody matters. Repeat it again, Diana. He doesn't matter.

She was in her car and driving away, the words still echoing in her mind. 'It doesn't matter,' she gritted between her teeth.

Diana spent the evening at home in a very depressed mood. She tried to force herself to relax, but she couldn't. She tried to concentrate on a book, and then some work in her briefcase, but she couldn't. She tried to keep her mind off of Alex, but she couldn't.

It had been such a brief encounter with him today, but it had upset her very much. She couldn't help but think of the coming week when she was supposed to spend most of the day with him. 'I can't handle this,' she told her tired face in the mirror. 'I really can't handle this.' She wondered if she should ask for a transfer to somewhere else, but rejected the idea as soon as she had thought it. Alex would ask why, or worse, he would know why, and she couldn't take that. No, she would have to stick it out. After all, as she had told him, she could take anything he could dish out. She ignored the little voice in her head that called her a liar, and climbed into bed. There was little rest for her that night.

CHAPTER SEVEN

'ALICIA Payne is here!' Carrie hissed at Diana when she walked into the office the next morning. The door was closed leading to the inner room and Diana eyed it doubtfully.

Her face brightened as she said with a hopefulness evident in her voice, 'Maybe Alex wants to talk to her alone and I should make myself scarce for a while.' But Carrie was shaking her head.

'Alex told me to tell you to go right on in whenever you arrived. He'll want to introduce you to her. I think she's here to try to convince him that she had nothing to do with that little fiasco a little while ago. The nerve of that girl! She'll lie through her teeth, and always with the most innocent look in those baby blue eyes. At least Alex knows what she's like. He can't possibly be fooled by her now,' Carrie finished speaking with a grim smile of satisfaction.

Diana tapped on the door lightly before walking in. The little scene that she walked into left her a bit more doubtful than Carrie. A slightly built woman was half perched on the side of Alex's big desk, her beautifully proportioned body posed to show the delightful curves to the fullest advantage. Her hair was a rare shade of reddish blonde that gave off rosy tints in the light. Her eyes, which turned briefly to the door, were indeed a very large and very limpid blue. Her face was heart-shaped and delicately boned, giving her an air of fragility that would arouse the most insensitive of men to a feeling of protectiveness. All in all, Diana thought wryly, she's a vision of angelical innocence.

Alicia had her small hands up to the tie at Alex's throat and was smoothing it into place with an intimacy that caused Diana's eyebrows and mouth to start to twitch. The female cat was establishing her claim to a territory in front of a strange adversary. Alex was watching Alicia with an enigmatic smile on his face. Diana watched the two of them and wished she was somewhere else.

Then Alicia was twisting off of the desk with a graceful move, and coming towards Diana with a warm smile. 'You've got to be Diana,' she said lightly. 'I'm Alicia Payne. You look every bit as pretty as I've heard everyone say.'

Diana smiled down at the charming face. 'Hello, Alicia. It's nice to meet you.' She looked up at Alex who had left his desk and had come around to stand by the two girls. 'Should I come back a little bit later?'

Alicia protested. 'Oh, don't go, Diana! I wouldn't want to be the one to send you out of your own office.' Now just what's that supposed to mean? she wondered. 'I was leaving soon anyway. I mainly wanted to come and invite you to a dinner party that I'm giving at the end of the week, Alex.' She turned to Diana. 'You, of course, are invited too. It will be fairly small, but formal, and everyone is expected around seven for cocktails.' She looked from one to the other with a pleading smile on her face. 'Oh, Diana, please say you'll come! Alex? You wouldn't let Diana go to a strange party all by herself, would you?'

He said lazily, 'That's blackmail, Alicia.' She gave a pretty pout. He turned to Diana, who raised her eyebrows enquiringly, but made no comment, leaving the decision to him. He asked Alicia, 'What day is the party?'

'Saturday. That way nobody will have to leave early because of work the next day,' she grinned.

'Well, if Diana would like to go, then I'll go, too.' Alex was watching her face.

'It sounds like fun,' she said, smiling and thinking no such thing. Alex's mouth twitched slightly. She knew he guessed what she was thinking.

'Good,' said Alicia with satisfaction, and Diana suddenly felt uneasy at the smile she gave. It looked like a cat who had got away with something it shouldn't have, and she wondered just what Alicia had planned for Saturday night. The girl was so charming that Diana had actually forgotten to keep up a wary guard around her. She watched Alicia talk to Alex excitedly about the party, and she made such a pretty and harmlessly friendly picture that Diana felt she was looking at a split personality. Alicia, when faced, was an enigma of contrasts. Diana felt a sudden revulsion towards the girl, almost as if she had been a snake.

She started to walk to her desk to set her briefcase down. Out of the corner of her eye, she saw Alicia reach up with one hand to caress the side of Alex's face gently. Diana felt a very strong urge to slap the hand away with a snarl, but managed to walk steadily to her desk and pretend to ignore it. She was amazed at herself; such a feeling of anger over something like that was new. She had never been possessive of anything or anyone in her life. She had always been the first to share or to give in school, and if someone had needed a loan of money, she never questioned, but gave what she could. To feel such a sudden wave of aggressive hostility towards someone else was startling to say the least.

Alicia was saying goodbye to Alex and she turned to Diana, saying with a friendly light in her eyes, 'I'm looking forward to Saturday, and the chance to get to know you better, Diana.' I'll bet! she thought, but she didn't comment. Then Alicia was gone with a wave of her hand.

The rest of the morning passed with what had become

unusual quietness. Alex seemed preoccupied and Diana, anxious to avoid any unnecessary confrontations, went out of her way to keep the peace intact. When she went out for her lunch break, she marvelled that the two of them had made it through a whole morning without any nasty scenes.

She was surprised to see the darkened office after her lunch break, for Alex usually stayed after she had left and came back before she did. She didn't see the dark silent figure behind the desk for a moment until her eyes got used to the darker room. Then, just as she had her hand out to flick on the light, she went rigid.

'Alex?' She spoke quietly. The dark figure in the chair moved a little and his voice came back as quietly.

'Yes?'

She moved into the room without touching the light switch. The closed curtains gave the room a shadowy effect, blurring greys upon greys, with the one black figure behind the desk.

Diana stopped uncertainly in front of the desk. She could see Alex a little better. He was sitting with both elbows resting on the desk top, hands laced with chin and mouth covered. She felt uneasy, unable to grasp his mood without the benefit of seeing his face.

'Do you have a headache? Would you like the light off for a while longer?' she asked, concerned.

'No, I'm all right.' But still the figure didn't move. She could only see dark shadows with a faint glitter where his eyes were supposed to be.

'Have you had any lunch yet?' she persisted.

'No.'

'I'd be glad to go down to the cafeteria to get you some sandwiches, if you like.'

'I'm not really hungry. Thank you anyway.'

Diana sat down in the chair that was pulled close to the

front of Alex's desk. This was not like Alex at all, and it worried her. He was usually so full of energy that he never wasted any part of the day, preferring instead to work right through his lunch hours and late into the evenings. She didn't know what he liked to do for relaxation, but this she knew was not right. She thought for a moment.

'You are thinking some problem through, aren't you?' she asked quietly. She could almost hear his smile.

'Something like that, yes,' he replied. There was such a lack of tension between them that Diana was unwilling to put on the harsh light or say anything to dispel the mood. This lack of strain had been how things were long ago. She felt a shock when she realised that only a week or two ago, this was how things had been between the two of them.

She decided to risk rejection, and asked carefully, 'Would you like to talk about it?' She tilted her head back and leaned comfortably into her seat as she waited for his reply.

He hesitated. 'No,' he said at last, and she felt somewhat disappointed. He continued, 'But it would be nice just to talk. Maybe it will help to clear some of the cobwebs in my mind and I'll be able to think about things with a fresh view.'

'All right,' she agreed. 'Would you like the light on?'

'No!' he spoke a little sharply. Then, more quietly, 'No, don't turn the light on. It's much too nice and relaxing like it is. I don't want this mood destroyed.'

Diana nodded in agreement, then realised that he couldn't see her. She said, 'I know what you mean. What would you like to talk about?'

The chair squeaked as Alex shifted. 'I don't know. Anything. Everything. Life, death, betrayal, love, hate.' Through his voice and in the pauses, she could hear the desk clock's tiny whir of electricity. 'You, me, them, anyone. What do you want to talk about?'

She chuckled, 'How about the latest weather updates?'

He gave a small groan. 'Anything but that! Surely we can find something, some interest we have in common?'

'We could always start with the first on your list,' she said lightly. She folded her hands behind her neck and crossed her ankles. 'How's life been treating you?'

'I don't know,' Alex spoke in a low voice. She frowned. It was a strange remark to make. 'Do you ever feel as if everything is going your way and then something happens and nothing is ever the same again?'

She sat very still. She knew what he meant, too well. As soon as she had met Alex, everything in her life had taken a sudden shift and she couldn't figure out just how it happened.

He was speaking. 'It seems like that's what happened to me and I don't know what I want any more or where I'm going. What do you want to do with your life, Diana?'

The question was unexpected and the surprise of it sent her mind racing, groping for an answer. She felt a jumbled mixture of emotions and she was at a loss to explain just why until it dawned on her. She sat quite still, lost in herself and her own revelation, and was almost unaware that Alex was listening, for he was so quiet. Then she heard herself speak, and realised as she talked that she was not answering the question for Alex. She was answering the question for herself. 'I think I want to do something worthwhile. I want to see something done and say, "Look, everyone, this is good. This is an achievement. I was able to do this thing."' She shifted restlessly. 'No, that isn't right, I don't know.' She stared at the ceiling. She tried to say that it didn't matter, that she wouldn't answer; she wanted to change the subject, but she couldn't. She needed the question answered. 'I want to fill an emptiness inside me with something good and worthwhile. I try to find it in everything that I do and everything

I dream. There's something inside me that's reaching out to a bright and shining ideal, only I can't seem to see where to go or how to reach it.' She repeated quietly, 'I don't know,' and wished she hadn't said anything. She felt naked.

Alex seemed to be listening intently to her little speech, and when she was through, he asked, trying to choose his words carefully, 'So you're searching for something but you don't know where to look or what you want to find?'

She sighed. 'Something like that, yes. It—it's as if it won't let me rest or stop trying to find it, I . . .' she faltered. 'Like I said, I don't know. Are you understanding any of this?'

He said very gently, 'Yes, I think I am. Once I felt like you did, but now I think I've found my ideal. I just don't know how to go about attaining it.'

'Oh,' she said eagerly, 'what is it?' He remained silent for a moment and as he started to speak she interrupted. 'No, don't tell me. I'm sorry. I didn't mean to pry.'

He told her quietly, 'I won't tell you now, Diana, but maybe someday, if I ever attain it, I will.'

'I'd like that,' she said hesitantly. Alex stood up and walked around the desk to her. He squatted down on his haunches in front of her chair and took her hands in between his. Twice he started to speak and stopped. Diana felt for some reason a little shaky and her heart was starting to pound.

'Diana,' he started, 'I want to apologise for the way I've treated you recently.' She started to speak, but he shushed her with a finger to her lips. 'No, hear me out. I have, for some odd reason, taken all my frustrations out on you, and attacked you in the most abominable way. There's no excuse for the way I've treated you, only the flimsy explanation that I can't even explain properly. Forgive me—I don't want to hurt anyone, and in spite of what you've said in the past, I feel I've hurt you.'

She couldn't control herself and tears started to run down her cheeks. This Alex was gentle, and while she was able to stand all his cold and hurting attitude, she couldn't stand this. She stayed silent, unable to speak.

Alex had to be able to feel the trembling in her hands as he gripped them, and his hands tightened fractionally. 'Diana—' he began. 'My dear, I hope you find your ideal. I want you to be happy, I want . . .' He took a deep breath. 'I wish you all the luck. If I can help you in any way, let me know.' She nodded, forgetting again that he couldn't see her, and he stood up, releasing her hands.

'I need to go and speak with Owen,' he said quietly. She knew he was giving her a bit of time to gather her control. 'I'll be back in half an hour, and I'll tell Carrie to hold all my calls.' He bent slightly and she felt his lips brush her forehead, and then he was gone.

Diana stayed where she was in the dark for a long time. She couldn't understand it, couldn't understand from where all of the pain and aching came. Everything was patched up between Alex and herself. Everything should be fine. Everything wasn't fine, and she felt the tears trickle one by one, wetting her face and hands.

By the time Alex had returned, she had herself under control and was working at her desk. But it was a precarious control, and there were slight smudges under her eyes and on her cheeks. Taking one keen look at her, he merely said cheerfully that he had got everything straightened out with Owen and that he'd sent down for some sandwiches for the two of them. Then he immediately sat down at his desk and was immersed in some papers. When the sandwiches came, they ate while still working and the afternoon was spent in a peaceful silence.

Nevertheless, Diana was more than glad to go home to

the empty silence of her apartment to soothe her raw nerves and try to relax.

The next day went as peacefully as the day before had, and in the afternoon, Alex sat back with a smile. 'This is very nice,' he commented, and Diana, looking up from her work, didn't pretend to misunderstand.

'It is, isn't it?' she agreed with a returning smile. It was beginning to feel like a joy to come to the office again, and not a chore to be endured.

'Are you busy tonight?' he asked suddenly, his gaze very blue and bright. They seemed to fairly sparkle in the cragginess of his features, and she stared, bemused.

Some of her old caution returned and she replied carefully, 'It really kind of depends, I suppose.'

He ran his fingers through his hair, tousling it wildly, and chuckled, 'Depends on what I have in mind, is that it?'

She laughed, 'Yes, I guess that is what I meant.' He didn't take offence.'

Instead, he asked with a grin, 'How good are you at roller-skating?' His eyes were definitely twinkling.

'Roller-skating?' she exclaimed. 'I've never been roller-skating in my life!'

'What?' It was a mild roar as he stared at her in surprise. 'You've never been roller-skating in your entire life?' She shook her head, smiling with amusement. 'Ever?' He evidently found it hard to believe. 'Would you like to go with me this evening, then?'

She was doubtful. 'I don't know,' she muttered. 'The floor always looks so hard.'

'You nut, it is hard.' Alex grinned at her in amusement. 'But if you go with me, you'll never take a spill.'

'How can you say a thing like that?' she scoffed at him in disbelief.

'I promise!'

'Promises!' Diana said bitterly as she picked herself up off the floor by pulling with her hands on the railing that surrounded the roller rink. 'I should have known better than to trust one of his promises! Especially one like that one was!'

Alex picked himself off the ground with more grace than she had. 'How was I to know you'd stick one of your big feet in front of mine?' he grumbled, gliding over with an ease that she eyed enviously.

'Of course you should know, I'm a novice!' she snapped testily. She rubbed her bottom. 'Boy, does my behind hurt!'

'Want me to massage it for you?' He grinned as he looked at her mischievously. She glowered at him sourly.

'No, thanks.' She shook her head sadly. 'I know a little girl who's going to be very sorry in the morning that she ever agreed to come to this fiasco. I wonder if she'll be able to make it to work.'

'I know a girl who's not so little, and that's why she's going to be hurting tomorrow,' Alex retorted as he grabbed her hands and prepared to take off again. Diana started to shriek protestingly. 'And,' he continued grimly, 'if she's not at work, she's going to be hurting more on her behind, and it won't be from falling! Oh, shut up, girl, and loosen up a little. I'm not going to let you fall, for heaven's sake! No! Don't do that—oh, hell—'

'Promises!' she grumbled, starting to crawl in the direction of the exit from the rink. 'See if I ever listen to your promises again!'

After an exhausting and hilarious hour on the rink, they called it quits, or rather, Diana refused to get up to fall again, and Alex in skates could not get the leverage to pick her up. They went out for coffee in a cute little restaurant and spent much of the time laughing over the disastrous attempts Diana had made on her skates.

He took her home late that night, and when they pulled up in the driveway, they kept talking, each reluctant to end the evening. He walked her to her door and she fumbled for her keys in the darkness. After locating them and inserting the key in the lock, Alex took over and opened the door for her, returning her key to her outstretched palm. She opened her mouth to say something, but he was first as he said softly, 'It's late, and we both get up early.'

She nodded, and there was a silence as they stared at each other. Her blood began to pound as she remembered the feel of Alex's arms, the pressure of his lips. He bent down and began to brush his lips by the side of her mouth and would have moved away, but she turned her face sharply and touched his lips with hers. They were softer than she remembered. He took in his breath hard, then his arms were around her and his lips weren't soft at all as he tightened them, bringing her close. She was trembling when he finally lifted his mouth away.

They looked at each other's faces. Alex's hand moved up to cup her chin and he watched her expression closely, slowly moving his head to hers for one final, deep kiss. He drew back, his breathing harsh and unsteady, and she reached up to touch his face with her hands. Alex sighed abruptly, muttering something incoherent to her as he took her hands in his and touched his lips to each before putting them away firmly. He pushed her hair off of her forehead in a rough movement as he whispered, 'Go inside, Diana. Now.' He turned away and Diana watched him get into his car and drive off.

She moved inside, her thoughts whirling chaotically around and around, uncomprehending her own responses to Alex's touch. She knew it was illogical to feel hurt, for she had rejected him and his concern for her, and yet somehow the situation was different. She felt the unreasoning emotion of a child who had been denied what he wanted.

She knew that it was what she was feeling; she told herself just that all night long. But it didn't stop her from crying bitter tears of frustration. 'Overreacting, my girl,' she muttered as she stared at herself in the bedroom mirror the next morning. 'Always overdoing it. Why can't you ever be in control?' A woebegone face looked mournfully back out of the mirror at Diana and shook her head. She skipped breakfast, taking instead two aspirins with her coffee.

She avoided Alex's gaze when she reached the office and limited her replies to monosyllables whenever possible. She felt stupid at the way she was acting, but couldn't seem to help herself. The strangest things began to bother her, and Carrie was alarmed to see her eyes fill with tears over a simple accident with the coffee.

'Are you all right, honey?' Carrie asked with concern as Diana dabbed at the spilled coffee on the table. 'You didn't burn yourself, did you?'

She shook her head and stared up at the ceiling for a moment, her eyes widened to avoid any tears spilling over and down her cheeks. 'No, I didn't burn myself,' she said huskily. 'I just had a bad night's rest and things seem to be bothering me today.' She looked at Carrie and managed to smile. Carrie's face relaxed slightly. 'Really, it was very stupid of me. I'm okay, seriously.' Carrie nodded, but she refrained from saying anything, and her eyes followed Diana around the room with a warm concern.

As the week went on, she could no longer use a bad night's rest as an excuse, but the sensitive mood would not desist. She felt frustrated at herself and tried desperately to stay in control, but this only made things worse. People began to treat her with a subtle but definite difference, being more kind and thoughtful than before, and more tolerant of her mistakes. One day there were flowers on her desk without a card, and the next day Jerry, the elevator boy, had a small box of candy for her. She felt very touched at these gestures of affection, but at the same time, she felt quite depressed. She had begun to think about putting in her resignation and looking for work elsewhere, and the reminders of people she had started to care about were tugging at her emotions, making her want to stay.

Still looming ahead was the dinner party on Saturday that had to be endured. Diana found herself brooding over it, wondering over and over again about the possible reasons Alicia had for inviting the two of them. There was one possible explanation that she came up with: Alicia wanted to make up with Alex and had prudently decided to try and pretend that she had no part in the vicious attacks on Mason Steel (thus, ultimately, on Alex). She mulled this thought over in her mind but then rejected it. A clever mind had been at work against Mason Steel, and to really think that Alex had not been fully aware of just who had been behind the whole set up was quite stupid. Only a fool would believe that there could ever be a chance to make up with Alex after that.

Diana went to Owen with her ideas and told him about the conclusions that she'd drawn. 'So Alicia could have only invited us for the foolish reason that she wanted to make thing up with Alex, or there must be a very smart reason for it. She wouldn't want to merely socialise— not with all that's happened,' she concluded, leaning back in her chair. Owen drummed his fingers on his desk.

'I think the one thing we can safely say is that Alicia is no fool,' he commented dryly.

'That's what worries me,' she sighed. 'I wanted to talk to someone who knew her to see if I was going crazy. This kind of thinking is really bizarre. I can't comprehend a mind that works like that.'

'For someone who can't comprehend a vengeful mind, you sure have an intuition for trouble,' chuckled Owen.

She smiled. 'It must be my feminine juices at flow,' she drawled. 'That girl makes my hackles rise!'

He looked sympathetic. 'I know what you mean,' he replied. 'That girl makes my hackles rise, and I hadn't even known that I had 'em to begin with!' They both laughed, but then he sobered. 'The damnedest thing of it is, Diana, you could be right. And if so, that leaves a very unpleasant question hovering around in my mind: what could she possibly have planned?'

She rubbed her eyes and shook her head. 'Don't ask me, Owen. My mind doesn't work like that!'

'I think you and Alex should cry off the night,' he spoke forcefully. 'You should just spend a nice quiet safely peaceful evening playing checkers or something, and forget that Alicia Payne ever existed.'

But she shook her head at that. 'No, whatever her nasty little mind has come up with, it can't really be all that dangerous. At least not physically, and we can handle anything else she sends our way. Besides, I'd kind of like to see just what she does have in mind. You know, sort of a sightseeing trip, and all that.'

Owen didn't smile this time. 'Just you be careful. Don't go and get yourself hurt.'

Diana spoke confidently, 'There's nothing Alicia could do to hurt me. Nothing!'

On Saturday afternoon, she began to rummage around in her closets and pull things out. Alex had offered to pick her up at six-thirty, which left her around two hours to get herself ready. She looked at what she had to wear and started to laugh. She had known what she was going to wear even before she'd pulled the different outfits out of the closet. She laid out the lavender dress with care and got out a pair of slender silver shoes to wear with it. She decided to pull her hair off to her face with two silver combs, leaving the back to fall in a chaotic mass of curls.

As she was preparing for the dinner party, Diana noticed in a vague way a darkening of light in her room. She impatiently flicked on the overhead lights and stopped. Going over to the window, she peered outdoors and gave a sigh of disgust. It looked like rain, the pallid grey of the earlier sky giving way to the darker clouds and turbulent purple streaks. The tree out by her front window swayed back and forth as a capricious wind tilted it first one way, then the next. There was no sign of the yellow golden sun of the previous weeks, and she was rueful as she contemplated the real end of summer and the beginning of fall. There was a heavy feeling to the air, lending an ominous cast to the rest of her preparations.

She was prompt and so was Alex, ringing the doorbell at exactly half past six. She let him in and went to put on a mid-length raincoat with a hood. She was unaware of the widening of Alex's eyes as he took in her appearance, or the glow of appreciation as he complimented her on her looks. She looked over her shoulder at his remark, belting the waist of the coat firmly. 'So you just like the dress, is that it?' she teased, and shook her head with a mock pout. 'And I spent all that time on my make-up for nothing!'

He laughed. 'I put the compliment badly, didn't I? Let me rephrase: Diana, I'm sure you'll be the loveliest woman at the dinner party tonight, because you're the loveliest woman in the world. No matter what you wear, how you dress, you would still be the most beautiful, because of who you are.' Shaking a finger at her, he leered, 'Of course, the dress doesn't hurt at all! Really, it's very, very nice!'

She sniffed and said sharply, 'It should be. They

charged me by the ounce!' A glow had started somewhere in the middle of her stomach and spread throughout her body at Alex's remark. She eyed him appreciatively. He was very tall and very formal in a black suit with a black tie, the severity of the outfit being broken only by a pair of heavy gold cufflinks and the stark white of his shirt. It made him look more powerful, emphasising the lean length of his legs and the width of his shoulders and bringing full attention to the strong vitality of his face, the rich brown and red glints to his hair and the vivid directness of his blue gaze.

He asked meekly, 'Will I pass?'

She laughed, nodding her head in affirmation.

'Just barely, but you'll do.'

'You little minx!' he growled.

'Not so little—my behind is still quite tender,' she chuckled as she locked the door and slipped the key into her small silver purse.

'You were smart to wear the raincoat,' Alex told her as he opened the car door for her and she climbed in. 'The forecast is pretty nasty for tonight—we may even want to leave the party early.'

'That bad?' she asked in surprise. 'I didn't know we were to expect such bad weather.'

'It really just developed this afternoon because of a freakish wind we've been getting today from the south-west. It is a little early for this kind of weather, though. The bad weather shouldn't be here until October or so.'

'South-west, did you say?' she asked, frowning. 'Isn't that tornado weather—winds from the south-west?'

'Only favourable conditions for one,' he replied calmly. 'It probably only means we'll have a bit of a messy night ahead of us.' He concentrated on his driving for a few minutes in silence, then asked, 'Are you worried at all, Diana? If you like, we could always turn back.'

'Oh, I'm not worried,' she said lightly. 'But I'll save the option for worrying until later on, if you don't mind. If it looks pretty rough outside, then maybe we could leave.' She hesitated, looking at his hands on the steering wheel. 'Alex?'

'Hmm?' He glanced sideways, a little smile tugging one side of his mouth awry. Diana didn't smile back.

'Are you—worried in any way about tonight?' Diana knew she sounded vague, but it was hard to articulate to Alex the way she did for Owen. Somehow, she felt foolish.

'In what way? The weather?' he asked slowly, frowning slightly.

'Oh no. I mean about the motives Alicia had for inviting us to the party tonight.' There was a pause. Diana finished, wishing she had kept her mouth shut, 'You know, I really don't think we'll be just socialising.'

He chuckled, 'I've given it a great deal of thought. That little girl has michief on her mind, I'm afraid. Just what, I don't know, but we should be on our guard tonight. She's going to pull something on us—on me, at least.'

'Well, you don't seem worried at all.' Diana was surprised.

'Curious, yes. Worried, not really,' he told her. 'Alicia just doesn't get me worried.' Ha! thought Diana. 'Now Derrick Payne is another matter. He's the vengeful son of a bitch that I'm going to watch tonight!'

Diana shook her head. She was sure that Alex was wrong about Alicia. He was underestimating her badly. Possibly he still believed a little in the sweet girl he had dated a while back who just got a bit too possessive for her own good. At any rate, Diana resolved to watch Alicia tonight. Derrick Payne was Alex's problem. She would deal with Alicia herself.

The sky was very dark by now and Alex put the car's headlights on. Everything was covered with the greyness that dusk brings, and Diana shivered. It seemed a cold, cold night, the kind of night that winter brings, without the comfort of the day's warm sun, the safe light shining on the land. Darkness is frightening, Diana mused, because of the unknown quality about it. We look out into the night from our safely lit windows and shudder at the thought of what might walk out there unseen. It's not knowing that's so unnerving about the blackness. Anything, anything at all could hide behind the veil of night. She shook off the mood of fancy and looked out her window with a fresh awareness. They were pulling into a long driveway with large trees that seemed to be maple on either side. The house was very large and well lit, with light streaming from big windows.

They reached the door and rang the bell, standing back while they waited, each in a withdrawn state and not looking at the other. Alex seemed to be affected by the heavy darkness as much as she. They heard footsteps in the hall inside, and then, as the door opened and a smiling servant greeted them, the skies opened up with a furious roar and wetness streamed torrentially down.

They stood looking out of the front door and marvelled that they had never got so much as a stitch of clothing wet, and the servant girl shut the door with an emphatic bang. 'Just in time, weren't you?' she asked cheerfully.

She took their coats and directed them into a very large and spacious room where a profusion of light and laughter spilled out. Diana got a blurred impression of a great many people, and thought to herself in disbelief, this is a small dinner party? Then Alex had a hold of her arm and was propelling her forward through the crowded room. Several times they were stopped by someone who knew Alex or knew of him, and any progress they made was painfully slow.

'Where are we going?' she hissed at him while smiling

and nodding to someone who seemed vaguely familiar.

'We're going to say hello to the host and hostess,' Alex murmured close to her ear. He waved in the direction of a voice hailing him, but kept going. Diana couldn't see any goal to his purposeful striding.

'I don't see them,' she whispered to him. 'Where are they?'

He nodded over to a big fireplace that was lit and roaring, and to the small group of people chattering close by. Diana could pick out Alicia, small though she was, but didn't know Derrick Payne to recognise him. 'Which one is Derrick?' she asked him quickly. They were fast approaching the group.

Alex looked at her and, with a smile that made them look as if they were talking about light, trivial matters when they really weren't, said softly, 'Do you see the large one over there right next to the fireplace, with the grey suit and the dark green tie?'

Diana looked and felt a bubble of laughter pop up from her stomach. The fellow was balding and fat, the large hands going to gesture with his conversation and returning to his belly to absentmindedly caress its width. She gurgled, 'Do you mean the bloated capitalist?'

Alex only had time to glance at Diana quickly, a light of laughter in the blue of his eyes, and then they were up to the group.

CHAPTER EIGHT

ALEX said smoothly, 'Good evening, Derrick, Alicia.' The group split and Alicia turned to face them, her face showing a startled surprise for an instant before smoothing over into a smile of delighted response.

Diana watched her closely and thought to herself, I bet she never expected us to show up. I bet she just came to Mason that day to see how much Alex suspected, and to see what she could get away with. Alex talked to Derrick for a moment and introduced Diana to him. She stayed silent, watching the two talk and the reactions of the group around her. Derrick was very nervous; it showed in the flutter of his fat fingers and in the way he answered Alex in quick-spoken sentences. The rest of the group was wary, everyone waiting to see how the meeting between the two men went before saying anything themselves. Alicia was looking from Alex to her father with a very tiny smile playing about her lips. She's enjoying this, Diana thought. Even though it's her own father who's so uncomfortable, that bitch is loving every minute of it.

Alicia turned to her suddenly. Her hair was piled high in careful little ringlets with a few escaping down her neck. She wore a very tiny black dress that had little up top, and slits up the sides. Her eyes looked very large and bright. She lifted one heavily jewelled hand up to her hair and patted it absentmindedly. Diana was reminded of Derrick's fat hands and had to quell a shudder. Alicia said, 'How nice of you to come, Diana.' She eyed Diana up and down, a sharpness in her eyes that hadn't been there before, the first time they met. 'You're looking so lovely tonight,' she cooed on. 'That dress is beautiful! And you have those lovely legs to carry it off, too.' Alicia fingered a necklace, one of many that she wore, and Diana remembered her own large and heavy silver bracelet that she wore on her right arm. It was the only piece of jewellery that she wore, bringing attention to the slender curve of her arm and giving the impression of something ethereal being chained to the heavy earth. Alicia looked at it too.

'Thank you, Alicia,' she said quietly, her eyes amused. 'You're looking very beautiful tonight, but then you were looking beautiful the first time I met you, too.'

Alicia preened a little, smoothing down the sides of her dress carefully. Diana wondered with distaste why she hadn't caught that particular mannerism the first time they had met. Alex turned to Diana and looked at her with eyebrows raised. Music had started up at the far end of the room and couples were beginning to dance. He hadn't spoken to Alicia since they had arrived.

Diana nodded with a smile and they drew together after murmuring excuses to the group, beginning to dance slowly. Both of them missed the sharp breath Alicia drew in at being so patently ignored or the way her eyes followed them through the entire dance, her eyes now very sharp and dagger-bright, noting everything. They didn't see Alicia's hands clench together in a spasm of uncontrolled fury, nor did they care.

Alex told Diana softly, 'After checking out every female in this room with all due consideration, I still hold you to being the most beautiful one here tonight.'

Diana snorted, a very inelegant sound. 'And you've had time to check out every female in the room? I bet you've carefully studied even the maids that are serving the drinks!'

Alex replied modestly, 'Well, I do try my best, you know.'

She muttered, 'I bet you do!'

He bent his head down to hers, his eyes very close and very amused. 'What was that you said?'

She was sure he heard every word of her muttered retort. 'Oh, never mind!' she replied, and felt his chest quake in a silent chuckle.

The dance was a slow and dreamy one, the music soft and mellow. Somehow Diana's head ended up on Alex's shoulder and his face rested against her hair; she never remembered just how it happened. Thinking about how hard it was to think about any business around Alex any more, she gave a great sigh, and his arms tightened.

'Now just what was that for?' He held her away from him to look down and ask.

'What was what for?' she asked, grinning at him. She knew what he had meant, but she had no intention of telling him the answer to his question.

'You know what I meant.' His mouth was pulled sideways in a cock-eyed smile that lent an easy charm to his features.

Diana opened her eyes very wide at that and pursed her lips, shaking her head. The dance ended and she stepped back.

Alex started to reply, 'You're just putting me off and I know it—'

'Why, hello there!' a man's voice boomed behind Diana. Her eyes widened in dismay as she recognised the owner of that voice and Alex had to smother a smile of amusement at the look on her face. She disguised it very quickly, though, and when she turned to greet Brent and Vanessa Valsing, she wore the most placid of looks.

'Mr and Mrs Valsing!' Diana exclaimed with every evidence of pleasure. Alex's polite smile of greeting to the Valsings widened perceptively. 'How good to see you again.' Diana shook hands with Brent first and then

Vanessa. 'But I thought you were in Kentucky for some reason.'

Vanessa replied with a smile that looked like it was painted on, 'I have family in Kentucky, but I don't remember telling anyone that we were going there in the near future.' She looked blankly at her husband, who shook his head.

'Oh,' said Diana. 'Well, that was probably what I heard and I'm remembering it wrong.' Everybody looked at each other. A thundering crash seemed to fairly shake the house and Diana jumped.

Vanessa laughed nervously. 'Oh, these storms you all seem to have around here! They're enough to scare the living daylights out of one, sometimes.' She gave a nervous giggle.

Diana moved over to a large window and stared outside. So far, it seemed to be all thunder and lightning and water. A bit noisy, maybe, and wet, but nothing to get really excited over yet. She looked at Alex and nodded. There was nothing to worry about right now.

They talked to the Valsings and as soon as possible made excuses to get away. Escaping to the other side of the room, Diana whispered to Alex, 'Whatever did she mean by "those storms we seem to get"—do you know?'

Alex shook his head. 'Nobody knows.' He caught sight of someone that he knew and whispered to her, 'Excuse me, will you?' and moved over to say something to him.

She stood watching people around her. She turned to pick up a glass that a maid offered to her politely when a voice spoke at her elbow. 'And are you having a good time, Miss . . . er—'

Diana swung around to see Derrick Payne. 'Carrington, Diana Carrington,' she supplied helpfully.

'Ah, yes. Miss Carrington,' Derrick Payne's little eyes had a dull expression in them, even though his lips were smiling. She was secretly repulsed, although she tried hard to hide it. 'How do like my home?' he rumbled, gesturing with a plump hand that was very pompous.

Smiling a little wider, Diana admitted honestly, 'I think it's really attractive, Mr Payne. Did your wife decorate the house?'

Something flickered in his eyes and was gone. Diana was unsure as to what it had been, the reaction had been so quick. It could have been merely a spark of intelligence, a look of surprise, a touch of—grief?

He replied, 'My wife decorated the house right after she gave birth to Alicia, twenty-four years ago. Since then, Alicia would have me redecorate in a more modern design, but I prefer it this way.' He looked about the room, then finished his drink in a few quick gulps. A maid passed by; he grabbed a fresh drink from her tray and at the same time deposited his empty glass. Diana's eyebrows shot up at the movement, for it had been amazingly quick for so large a person. Derrick Payne continued, 'She passed away shortly afterwards, but of course you would have heard of that.'

Diana worked the information around in her mind. She now thought she knew what the look had been on Derrick's face; it had been a look of anger. He had assumed that Diana knew of his wife's death and had mentioned her out of tactlessness or malice. After standing still for a moment, Diana made a short quick movement with one hand. The heavy bracelet winked in the light; she looked at it. She said very quietly, 'I'm sorry, Mr Payne. I didn't know. It was stupid of me.'

He glanced at her and then away. 'Quite all right, my dear. It was a long time ago.' His other drink was almost gone and he finished it quickly. A dull flush was beginning to show on his face and around the loose jowls. He said suddenly, abruptly, 'Maybe it was better things have happened the way they have and Charlotte died at the time she did. She would have been unhappy now, I think.'. He didn't look at Diana. There was a pause in the midst of all the chattering and laughter that came from various parts of the room and from different groups. 'Would you like to see my collection of antique china, Miss Carrington? My wife was very proud of it.'

Diana smiled, this time with pleasure. 'I would like that, Mr Payne.'

They made their way into another room, a much smaller room this time, with ornate rugs on the hardwood floor and two large couches in the middle. To the right were several large glass cabinets, light bouncing off the gleaming and polished front. Derrick led Diana to the first one and began to explain the pieces of china that were propped inside. Diana was extremely interested and for the duration of Derrick Payne's little talk, remained silent except for a few intelligent questions. After chatting for a while, they began to head back to the large party room where the rest of the guests were.

On the way back, Derrick Payne suddenly asked, 'Tell me, Miss Carrington, how are things going for you at Mason Steel? Are you liking your work there?'

Diana felt a bit wary and answered carefully, 'I'm finding the work very hard, of course, but I like it better than anything I've ever done before. I'm very lucky— luckier than most people, I think, because I'm in the unique position of power where I'm enough of my own boss to satisfy my independence, and yet not be burdened down with the heavy responsibility of ownership.'

Derrick nodded ponderously. 'You seem to handle your responsibilities well, too. I hear that it's largely through your quick intervention that Mason Steel was able to make it through the . . . ah, rough times in the past.' It was the closest he had ever come to speaking to Diana about the price war that occupied so much of her time in the weeks before.

Diana felt a slight shock of realisation that she had just spent a surprisingly pleasant half-hour with the man who had been responsible for the near ruin of Mason Steel. Payne's remark immediately put her on guard as she intuitively guessed that he was much more complex than the 'bloated capitalist' she had so blithely assumed.

Modesty was the better part of valour, she decided. 'Oh, I daresay they would have made it through without me,' she replied, smiling slightly.

Derrick was watching her closely out of little pig-like eyes. 'But yet you were the one who assumed the responsible role and pulled things together. I like that; it shows a rare talent.' I bet, Diana thought. 'In fact, I admire it so much that I'm eager to get people like you involved on my own staff.' He rocked a little on his heels, drumming his sides with his fingers. 'Just to let you know, my dear, if you're ever in need of a job, just come to me. I guarantee you a position of responsibility any time you like. I'm even willing to consider a raise in salary up to twice that of your present pay.'

Diana had to suppress a cry of astonishment at Derrick's words. In the end, all she managed to get out was, 'Oh, Mr Payne, you don't know what ridiculously high wages I'm getting now. In fact, my last raise was quite extraordinary. Too much, I thought.' The amusement that she felt at Derrick's amazing proposition died and she continued quite hardly, 'Besides, loyalty can't really be bought, not with money.'

There was a silence as they both eyed each other. Derrick's eyes were narrowed; Diana's were cold. He bowed slightly and said with a note of mockery that had not been apparent in his voice before, 'Thank you, Miss

Carrington, for a most pleasant interlude.' He turned and walked away.

Diana stared after him with a bemused expression. She realised now that the only reason Derrick Payne had invited her to the other room had been to discuss the possibility of her allegiance taking a major switch from one employer to another.

She started as a voice sounded right beside her left ear. 'And what was that all about?' Alex asked softly, his eyes following Derrick's movements across the room with a shade of suspicion.

Diana turned. 'I think,' she said, 'I've just been bribed.'

Alex hissed, sucking in his breath sharply. His eyes narrowed in anger, then swivelled to take in her expression. 'And might I ask the outcome of the little talk?' he enquired quietly.

Diana felt a surge of hurt and anger. Her eyes flashed as she retorted. 'Good lord, Alex, do you even have to ask?' She then pivoted on her heel and jerked away quickly, intent on putting as much distance between herself and Alex as possible. He started to follow, but jerked to a momentary halt as Alicia announced to the room in general that the buffet dinner would be starting in the next room and for everyone to help themselves.

Diana had turned at her announcement, as had everyone else in the room, and she was just in time to see Alicia put her hand on Alex's arm and say something sweetly up into his face. Alex looked at Diana frowningly, but she had already looked away by then, a nagging pain in her chest at the sight of Alicia and Alex together. She smiled with a great deal of warmth at a young man whom she had vaguely recognised earlier, but couldn't put a name to, and he came towards her with a wide smile.

Alex watched Diana for a moment as she talked with the young man with every sign of enthusiasm, then turned to Alicia. He offered Alicia his arm and she took it promptly. There was a secret smile of satisfaction that hovered around her lips, but Alex didn't notice.

The dinner was long and leisurely as guests wandered in and out of the three tables at random, selecting their food and carrying their plates to the other side of the large room and taking their pick of seats at the several tables set up. Diana looked at the wide choice of foods laid out before her and felt slightly sick at the thought of eating. There was a large crash of thunder outside, louder than any previously, making people jump. The sky was pitch black and the wind furious as it whipped around the house, whistling eerily. There was some nervous laughter as the different people who had jumped looked around with some degree of embarrassment.

Diana, moving to the nearest window and looking out, thought to herself, 'This is really getting bad. It looks dangerous out tonight.'

Alex started to move after her, but Alicia said something else to him, her lips pouting prettily. He turned back, and Diana looked away from the window, searching for him with her eyes only to see an apparently unconcerned Alex laughing down at Alicia as she led him to the first table laden with delicacies.

Diana found the young man (she was too embarrassed to ask his name) right beside her, eyes admiring and apparently ready to devote his time to her, and she shrugged. Why not? It was better than eating alone and she was sure as hell not going to sit with Alex if it meant sitting with that bitch.

The young man carried Diana's plate to a seat a little distance away from Alicia and Alex and set it down carefully. He asked her charmingly, 'Would you like something to drink?'

Diana smiled. It was a pity she couldn't remember his

name, for he seemed like a nice young man. 'That really would be nice, yes.'

He grinned at her. 'I'll be right back.'

She spent most of the dinner watching Alex and Alicia and trying to come up with suitable replies for the young man's chatter, which afterwards she couldn't remember a thing about. Time seemed to drag on for an eternity, almost as if it were standing still. Diana puzzled this over vaguely, shaking herself out of her daydreams when the young man spoke her name.

'What? I'm sorry, I was miles away,' she said apologetically. He was wearing a very patient look on his face and she got the uncomfortable feeling that he had spoken her name more than once.

'I asked you if you'd like some more punch. There's some intriguing red stuff over in that punch bowl on the second table, and I'd be glad to get you some,' he repeated. Diana got the impression that he was as anxious for the night to end as she was.

'That would be fine,' she replied. He got up from the seat with alacrity, grabbed her half-empty glass of punch and headed for the table. Diana had to smile wryly.

There was a minor commotion over at the other table and her eyes travelled to it. Her eyes sharpened as she saw Alex leap to his feet and start to dab at his front while Alicia stood wringing her hands and alternately wiping at her dress front and then at his white shirt and black coat. A red stain was oozing rapidly on the shirt, showing up like blood vivid against what little white was left. Diana's eyebrows twitched. Alicia seemed to be talking very fast, but Diana couldn't hear her. She was looking up into Alex's face with a pleading look and he made a dismissive gesture while dabbing at his shirt with a sodden and stained napkin.

The young man came back, grinning from ear to ear.

'Looks like Alicia slipped up,' he stated with every sign o'
satisfaction.

Diana laughed. 'Is she the one that spilled the punch?'
she chuckled.

'Yes, although it's unlike her to go and get punch for
herself,' he replied maliciously. 'She must have spilled it
because she's out of practice. She usually has someone else
get it for her.'

She fumbled for her napkin to dab at her mouth and try
to hide her face. The young man's voice had a slight note
of pique in it, if she was not mistaken. Once upon a time
he must have been one to fetch and carry for Alicia. She
looked down at the punch that she didn't want, her eyes
dancing. He certainly seemed to have a talent for it!

Across the room, Alicia and Alex were headed for the
door that led to the stairs in the hall. Diana saw Alicia
motion Alex on ahead, then stop to whisper something to
a maid who was standing by the door. Then she disappeared out of the room as well.

Diana guessed they were going to clean up and went
back to her meal. A crash of thunder echoed as a flash of
lightning sent everyone blinking. The young man exclaimed with a large grin (Diana wished he would stop
smiling so much; it was getting on her nerves), 'Golly, that
was close!'

'I'll say!' Derrick moved to the window, his face furious.
'It hit in the back yard and probably killed that big old oak
over there!' People moved to the window to murmur and
exclaim, the young man moving with them. Diana laid
down her napkin, hearing someone farther down the room
ask plaintively, 'What does an oak tree look like?' There
was a general round of laughter at this remark.

Diana sensed someone at her elbow and she looked
around in surprise to see the maid that Alicia had spoken
to before going upstairs to change.

She smiled up at the young girl as she began to speak. 'Miss Carrington?'

'Yes?' Diana replied.

The girl hesitated. Then she said, 'I'm to tell you that Mr Mason is in the room three doors to your left as you climb the front staircase, if you would like to go and talk with him about leaving early because of the accident.'

She frowned. 'How stupid of me! I never thought of that. Of course he would want to leave early since he has nothing to change into.' She looked up at the girl in puzzlement. 'Did he send you down here?'

'No, ma'am, Miss Payne did just before she went upstairs to change too,' the girl replied politely.

Diana hesitated, sensing something but not really understanding. She said finally, 'Thank you. Maybe I should go up to talk to him.'

The maid murmured something and backed away to go and start picking up abandoned and empty plates and glasses. Diana looked around to see if she could locate the young man that she had spent the dinner with and saw him over in a small group of people by the windows, still staring outside and chattering. He didn't appear to be in a hurry to come back, so Diana shrugged her shoulders and didn't take the trouble to go over and make her excuses.

She picked up her half-empty plate and carried it over to where the servants were gathered, beside two serving carts, and gave one of them her plate with a thanks. She stood by the maid who had delivered the message and asked, 'It was the third room on the left?'

She turned and nodded. 'Yes, ma'am. You're to go on in.'

Diana's brow wrinkled in perplexity. What a strange thing to say! She turned and left the room, crossing over to the stairs.

The sounds of the storm were louder as she moved away

from the noise and the laughter of the crowded room and made her way up the staircase. The howling fury had increased. Diana thought it was a good thing that they were leaving soon anyway. She thought back on the route they had travelled earlier and shuddered. There were a few winding roads that would be hairy to negotiate in this kind of weather, and she was glad it was Alex who had driven and not her. He was the better driver.

The second floor hall was carpeted with a luxurious thick mat of heavy shag, and Diana made no noise as she walked down its length. She looked about her; a fortune had gone into the carpeting alone, not counting the antique pieces filling the house. Then, counting the doors on her left, she stopped in front of the third door.

She tapped lightly. 'Alex?' she called as she turned the doorknob and opened the door. 'They told me to come on in—' There she stopped short, hanging on to the doorknob as if it were a lifeline. A blow seemed to come from nowhere and strike at her stomach as she took in the scene meeting her eyes. She closed them, gasping harshly, the sound loud in the sudden quiet. Then a very bright lightning flash made her open them on reflex as it lit the room into a cruel clarity.

Alex and Alicia were in the room. Alex's chest was bare and so was Alicia's. Alicia's little black dress was about halfway to her waist and her hair tumbled down her back in a cascade of curls. Her hands were in the arrested action of caressing Alex's bare chest.

They both had turned their heads sharply at Diana's entrance, Alex sucking in his breath and Alicia jerking her hands to cover her breasts, an obscure look on her face. Diana's eyes took in an open door at the other side of the room that led to another room, but she didn't comprehend any more anything that she saw.

A sudden fit of violent trembling hit her as she closed

her mouth and covered its vulnerability with one hand. She raised the other hand, visibly shaking, as if to ward off the sight of the two together. There was a moment of stunned silence, then she whispered behind her hand and shook her head, mumbling, 'I'm sorry—my mistake.'

Then she was away from the door, pulling it shut behind her and running down the hall to the stairs, tears coursing down her face. She didn't notice them fall; she didn't notice anything but Alex's shout behind her and her own churning stomach.

'Diana! Damn it, Diana!' he roared after throwing the door open and standing in the doorway. Diana, however, didn't look back as she stumbled at the top of the stairs and hurried down. She heard a sound she was never to forget. It came from behind her, incredibly horribly echoing in her mind long after she had got away and out of range. It was the sound of Alicia's laughter, light and amused, as she chortled her triumph and satisfaction. Diana shook her head numbly. It was impossible to feel any more pain.

A maid was in the hall, her startled face swivelling to the sounds of Diana's erratic footsteps on the stairs and taking in her obvious distress.

Diana whispered urgently, 'Bathroom?' Nausea was hitting her in waves.

The girl pointed to the other side of the hall and to her left, saying something that Diana didn't take in as she rushed past.

She opened a door and saw the small interior of a half-bath, slamming the door and locking it behind her, cursing furiously at her trembling and ineffective hands, then she was violently, painfully sick, retching long after her stomach was empty and crying helplessly. Afterwards, she sat on the floor in an exhausted heap, leaning her head against the wall with close eyes.

Footsteps sounded just outside the bathroom door, but Diana didn't hear them and she jumped, moving back against the wall in a gesture of fear as she heard Alex's voice.

'Diana?' he asked quietly. The doorknob moved as he tested it and found it locked. She watched the movement with a horrified fascination. She couldn't remember locking it. 'Diana, are you in there?'

Now she could remember locking the door. She wrinkled her brow as she tried to make her mind think. It was as if the whole world was in cotton, and she couldn't seem to function. It was upsetting her very much, for her mind was one thing she prided herself on, and the ability to think. This must be what shock does to one, she thought. Her hands were shaking very violently, and had been, as she recalled, when she had tried to grasp the latch. She raised them and looked at the veins. 'Diana!' Alex called. His knuckles rapped the door and his voice was sharp with worry. Her hands blurred in front of her as her eyes filled. She tried to clasp them together. Concentrate on survival, she whispered, hugging herself. That's all that's important, the only thing that's important. Survive. She felt a great jolt as she realised that she hadn't whispered the words after all. 'Are you in there?' Alex's voice was raised and he shouted, 'Damn it Diana, are you all right?'

Her head turned at that. Am I all right? she thought, her lips twisted in what was supposed to be a smile. Oh, God, he asks if I'm all right! She dragged herself to her feet and lurched to the basin and the mirror behind it on the wall. She ignored the pounding and shouts coming from the other side of the door and looked at the pale wreck of a human being in the mirror. 'So,' she whispered, and this time was pleased to hear a sound coming from the lips of the person looking out at her. 'You heard the man. Are you all right?' The girl in the mirror blurred as her hands had done, and she cried out silently, Be all right, damn it! You must! You must!

She turned on the cold water and began to splash her face and slap it, uncaring of the hurt she inflicted. It couldn't hurt on the surface any more than it did inside. After getting a little colour back on her cheeks, she took out her silver combs and combed her hair into some semblance of order, then replaced the combs in her hair. She took her time, oblivious to anything else but the fact that somehow she had to present herself to be intact and not the shattered mess she felt herself to be. She didn't analyse; she was beyond realising just what had made her react the way she had. All she was aware of was that animal instinct, that determination to survive.

She finished her tidying up and moved to unlock the door. She opened it to face a pale Alex, eyes flashing vividly and furiously as he raked his hair back with one shaking hand. A maid hovered in the background, her face anxious and concerned. Diana looked at her and managed a smile, albeit a wobbly one. She had been the one to direct Diana to the bathroom, and, she guessed, the one to direct Alex to her too.

The maid smiled uncertainly back and then scuttled away; now that Diana was out of the bathroom, she was intent on getting lost.

Diana's eyes swivelled to Alex. She took in his crisp white shirt, rolled at the elbows, with surprise. 'Where did you get the clean shirt?' she asked curiously.

He sucked in his breath, searching her face intently. 'Derrick and Alicia seemed to have my size in stock,' he said harshly, and continued, 'Diana, let me explain what was going—'

She interrupted him desperately, 'I don't want an explanation of what was going on. I made a gross mistake, let's leave it at that. All I want is to—'

'Dammit, you're going to listen to me!' he snarled, lips
tight against his teeth. He grabbed her by the arms and
hauled her up against his chest. At this, she struggled so
furiously that he was forced to loosen his grip a little to
avoid hurting her. Voices sounded close by as a few people
approached from down the hall.

Diana twisted hard and was suddenly free. She said, not
looking at him as she rubbed her arms, 'It's very nasty
out.' She spoke in a dull, flat voice. 'I think we'd better go
now.' They stood rigid and still as the people came into
view.

Alex moved, a jerky and impatient gesture at the
interruption. 'All right,' he whispered. Only Diana could
catch his words. 'We'll leave. But we aren't through, no,
by a long shot, and you're going to listen to me tonight one
way or another!'

CHAPTER NINE

DIANA avoided Alex's eyes as they collected their coats. She went through the motions of putting on her coat and belting it, unaware of her surroundings or what she was doing. She kept wishing over and over that the evening would end and that she would have time to lick her wounds in private.

Alex took her arm and led her outside. They both instinctively flinched when the fury of the storm lashed and tore at them, whipping their coats around their legs. He propelled Diana into a run and after opening the passenger door, thrust her inside. Then he hurried to the other side and got in quickly, slamming the door behind him. They didn't speak to each other as he started the car, reversed down the driveway and drove out on to the street. The darkness was a madness that howled and screamed as it whirled about the car, seemingly to try to reach the two sheltered in the car.

Alex started to speak. 'Diana . . .'

'Don't!' she said sharply. 'Can't you see? I don't want to hear it.'

The fingers on the steering wheel started to tighten until his knuckles were white and strained. 'You've got to listen to me,' he spoke quietly in an effort to stay calm. 'Alicia had just come into the room because she needed—'

'Stop it!' Diana put her hands over her ears, trying to block out his words. 'I won't listen to you!'

'For once in your life, damn it, you're going to have to!' he snapped intensely. She shrank back in her seat. 'Nothing happened, for God's sake! If you'd just sit still for a minute, I'll—'

'Will you shut up!' Diana's voice rose as she tried to drown out his words. 'I don't care what did or did not happen! It's none of my business!'

Alex held the car on the road, swearing while he fought the buffeting winds that grabbed at the car and jerked it from side to side. The tyres gripped the pavement and he relaxed slightly, beginning to speak. 'It is your business, Diana, whether you want it to be or not.' His face was hard, his voice implacable. 'Your reaction tells me that much at least—'

'Shut up!' Diana's eyes overflowed and tears splashed down her cheeks. She stared at him, but failed to see through the wetness blinding her. 'I will not listen to this! I will not . . .'

She started to fumble at the car door latch, not really comprehending her own actions but intent only on getting away from Alex and his painful insistence. He glanced over to her and grabbed her hands with one of his.

'What the hell do you think you're doing!' he shouted. His face was white, his eyes burning with an inner fire. She began to struggle with him, fighting to free her hand with a desperation and strength that he found hard to control. 'Diana, stop! Sit back and put your safety belt on, now!'

She sobbed, 'No! No, just leave me alone, I can't take this. Will you let go of me?' She flung this as she managed to wrench her hand away and pushed at his arm. 'Damn you, when will you let me be?'

Alex's attention had been diverted from the road and when headlights flared suddenly in their path, he jerked his eyes back in front of him and started to wrench the steering wheel hard to the right in an effort to miss the oncoming car. The headlights in front of them swerved crazily and drunkenly as they blinded Alex and Diana. She sat frozen, horrified and panic-stricken as she stared right into the glaring light. Alex, trying desperately to stop some of their momentum, slammed on the brakes while battling the wheel, but the tyres refused to hold on the pavement and the car began a sickening, out-of-control skid. Diana felt a great lurch as the car left the road and the bottom of her stomach seemed to plummet as the car fell, fell, then there was the screaming and tearing of crumpling metal, a shattering of glass, and a hard, hard blow.

Diana felt a wetness dripping down her face and seeping into her clothes. It was as if the world was crying, crying with a deep sorrow over the brokenness, the tragedy . . . With a supreme effort, she managed to force open her eyes after failing the first attempt. Getting her eyelids open a crack, she saw nothing at first. Sobbing with fear and pain, she opened them a little wider and realised that the darkness was not a complete blackness, but instead was made up of shadows of the night. The wetness was indeed a gentle rain that pattered on her face and covered the outside ground with innumerable puddles, the earlier storm having abated.

She looked around as she began to comprehend that she was indeed outside, part of her body being pinned under the heavy and numbing weight of the car. She felt the wet metal of the car with her hands as she tried to make out in the darkness what part held her pinned and realised that she must have been thrown out of the front of the car, through the broken windshield, for the front was what held her.

She looked up the side of the long, deep ditch and saw the other car perched half off the road on its side, its lights now dead and frighteningly dark. All around her was the terrifying and telling silence, implying that which she could not accept.

Diana tried to call out, but a pain in her chest prevented any sound louder than a feeble hoarse whisper. She coughed hard, spitting out something dark and wet and crying helplessly, for the pain was beginning to hit her in overwhelming waves.

'Alex?' she whispered. She rolled her head from side to side, trying to see better. 'Somebody? Anybody? Oh, dear God, help me, please! It hurts. Alex?'

Then she saw the still dark figure that was still in the car and she stared at it in horror. It was a sight that was to haunt her dreams and waking thoughts for years. 'Alex?' she called softly. She held out her hands to it and whimpered. Dark sticky fluid was on her arms and hands, oozing out and running down her arms as it mingled with the rain.

Pain hit her like a sledgehammer then, and she screamed over and over again. 'Alex!' she cried out once more, then passed out.

Vague and fuzzy lights seemed to be bobbing up and down just beyond Diana's eyelids and she flickered them open briefly. There were flashing lights up on the road that looked to be ambulances. Men were all over the slope where the two cars were and several came running towards her. She whispered, 'Alex?'

One of them turned and shouted, 'We have a girl over here alive! She's trapped under the car—hurry!'

She tried again to ask about Alex, but her voice wouldn't come out past her throat, which was swollen. The man who had shouted to the others turned back and bent down to stroke the wet and tangled hair off her forehead. He said gently, 'Hold on, honey. Help is on the way now. Just hold on.'

Tears started to stream down her face as she tried to speak. She couldn't make him understand, make him turn and look into the car at that horribly still figure. He crooned to her, 'Don't try to talk now. Don't hurt yourself. Everything will be all right.'

Diana raised a shaking and bloody hand to point tremblingly at the front of the car, but the man didn't look as he focused intently on her, feeling for her wrist for her pulse. He said, 'We'll have the car off very soon. I know it hurts, but we've got some medicine and it'll help the pain.'

She moaned, sobbing now, and shook her free hand at the car. The man glanced at it, then shouted in astonishment, 'Oh, my God! There's a person in the car still! Quick, he might be alive!'

She couldn't keep her eyes open any longer and with a final sob of fear and pain, she relaxed once again unconscious.

When she finally opened her eyes again, all she saw was white. With an effort, she managed to bring things into focus and realised that she was in a room. Turning her head from side to side, she was able to see the bars on either side of her bed and see the stand by the bed laden with flowers, different vials and bottles and a phone. She relaxed her head on the pillow, sighing. 'I really am an idiot,' she thought. 'Of course, I'm in a hospital.' This thought brought back the rest of her memory of that black night and she scrabbled frantically around for a buzzer of some sort to call a nurse.

As she was searching desperately, the door to her right opened to admit a starched and white figure who hurried to her side when she saw her conscious and in great distress. Hands grabbed at Diana's and the figure spoke. 'What is it, honey? What did you need? Are you in pain? Here, see, this is the buzzer to press if you need anything, is that what you were looking for?' The nurse shoved a small box-like object into Diana's hands. 'What's wrong, dear?'

'Alex?' she whispered weakly. 'Alex?' Tears started to drip down her cheeks as she began to cry. She was certain he was dead. That still form in the crashed car had been too real.

'Alex Mason?' the nurse asked. Diana nodded rapidly. 'He's just fine, Diana. Don't you worry about a thing. Alex is fine.'

She sobbed, 'You're lying, lying. He was hurt badly. I could see him in the car so still. He's dead, isn't he? I know!' The nurse started to say something soothingly, but Diana screamed at her, 'Isn't he?'

The nurse pushed a button and someone came in carrying an object that Diana couldn't see. Then, as her arm was held by the first person who tried to soothe her, the other person jabbed the arm with a sharp needle and she sobbed despairingly as the room whirled and grew dark.

Grace was sitting in a comfortable chair when she whispered, 'Hello, Grace.'

She looked immediately. Quickly getting to her feet, she moved over to the bed and put a cool hand on Diana's hot forehead. 'Diana—how do you feel, darling? Does it hurt much? I can get you a nurse if you need one.'

Diana shook her head weakly. The pain was bad, but it was bearable. She asked, 'Tell me about Alex, please, Grace.'

Grace shook her head in return and replied, 'Alex is doing really well. Don't you worry about him. You worry about yourself and getting better.'

Diana closed her eyes. 'Grace, don't lie to me. Was Alex hurt in the accident?'

Grace hesitated and Diana's eyes flew to her face to stare at her hard. 'Yes, he was,' Grace said finally. 'He was hurt pretty badly, worse than you were. At first, after surgery, they weren't sure that he would live, but he made it through the night and he's been improving ever since.'

'Ever since?' she asked, shocked. 'How long has it been since Saturday?'

Grace smoothed the hair off of Diana's forehead. She said gently, 'Four days. It's Wednesday, my dear.'

She sighed, 'Good God!' Her eyes sought Grace's, her expression begging for reassurance. 'Will he be all right now? How was he hurt—will he recover? Completely, I mean?'

Grace spoke wryly, 'I shouldn't be telling you all this, you know. Upsetting the patient, and all.' Diana grabbed her hand impatiently.

'You probably shouldn't be—but Grace, you can't stop now. Damn it, you just cant!'

She nodded, her lined face sympathetic. 'I know, my dear. I've said too much already. He was hurt internally pretty badly, with a couple of broken ribs and some bleeding. He got a nasty concussion and a few cuts on his face that are pretty minor. The problem was when the doctors found out that one of his ribs had pierced the lung cavity.'

Diana sucked in her breath, wincing in pain. 'But he will be okay—you said that? He'll be all right?'

Grace took her hands and pressed them with her own. 'He should be all right.' She put the emphasis on the word 'should'. 'They think he's out of danger now, but they're still watching him closely for a while longer before moving him out of intensive care. The danger is that he might develop pneumonia, which would be disastrous with his perforated lung.'

Diana relaxed a little on her pillows. 'He'll be all right, Grace. Just you wait and see, he'll be all right.' It was spoken with a note of desperation as her eyes looked to Grace for strength.

Grace nodded, speaking firmly. 'Of course he'll be all right!' She smiled down at Diana's poor bruised face. 'You haven't even asked about yourself yet. Don't you want to know how you are?'

Diana grimaced. 'If it's anything like I feel, I'm not sure I want to hear it! I feel awful.'

Grace smoothed the pillows on the bed and bustled about doing odd jobs in the room. She spoke cheerfully. 'You were the lucky one. You'd been trapped under the car as it had fallen, but its fall had been broken by several large rocks that were all around you and they kept you alive. Otherwise, the weight of the car would have killed you almost certainly.' Oh, great! Diana thought. Grace came around and stared down into her face. She spoke very seriously now. 'Diana, we've all been thanking God for the miraculous way you were saved. Of course,' she continued, trying to make light of Diana's injuries so as not to worry her, 'your poor legs were broken and your body was banged around badly. You'll probably have the sniffles from being out in the rain for so long, but otherwise, you'll be just fine!'

Diana nodded, feeling suddenly very tired and sleepy. 'What about my arms and face? Why do I have bandages on them? I can't seem to remember.'

Grace replied, 'You just got some superficial scratches from the windshield shattering. There won't be scars.'

'And Mason Steel?' she mumbled, trying to stay awake to hear Grace's answer.

'For heaven's sake, don't think about it now! Everything's fine, and all you have to worry about is falling asleep for a little nap . . .' Grace looked down at Diana's closed eyes as she softly ended and tiptoed out of the room.

Diana had a very long time to herself in the next few

days in which all she had to do was think. She couldn't seem to keep her mind away from the horrible scene in the bedroom at the Paynes' and she couldn't block out the horror of the accident. Later on she was told by one of the doctors that it had been a drunken driver in the other car who had crossed the meridian and had caused their crash. He had not survived.

Diana couldn't help the jumble of thoughts that kept tumbling through her head. She thought quite a bit about Alex, morbidly imagining him dead in the car, a still dark figure that would never move again. She had different pictures of him flash through her head. She remembered the talks that they had shared and the fun times together. She remembered how it felt to have his lips hard and pressing on hers, and the feel of his arms surrounding her and holding her so close. She imagined him caressing Alicia and felt sick to her stomach.

The next day, a nurse came into Diana's room and told her with a smile that Alex had been conscious in the night and had asked about her. Diana felt the ready tears of weakness and relief wash away her fears as she heard the news. Over and over, she thanked God that Alex was alive. Later on in the day, she asked for a mirror to see her face. The nurse was reluctant to give in, but after much cajoling and arguing, was persuaded to find a mirror. Diana was prepared for a bruised face, but she was shocked at the battered and scratched visage that met her eyes when she peered into the mirror. Touching her cheek with one bandaged hand, she stared soberly at herself. 'You were lucky, my girl,' she told the apparition. 'Both you and Alex were.'

She went into a deep depression soon afterwards. She began to think of the future and what she would do when she was released from the hospital, but all she could envision was a great blackness ahead of her. There was no possibility of her going back to work for Mason Steel, of that she was sure. Too much had happened. She couldn't face the thought of working day after day in such close contact with Alex, always torn between jealously wondering who Alex might be seeing, taking out or—she forced herself to say it—touching, and the fierce desire to touch him herself.

With these thoughts, Diana's breathing stilled as she considered the implications of what her jealousy meant. The truth hit her with such a terrific clarity that she put her hands up to her head and groaned in anguish. It was so obvious, so incredibly obvious that she was amazed at her own stupidity in not realising it before.

She was in love with Alex.

Realising the truth about oneself is not always easy or pleasant, and Diana was certainly not an exception.

She began to see herself differently from what she had before. She had considered the attraction she felt for Alex a threat to her own strength of personality. Now she realised that it was herself that she was afraid of. She was afraid of getting hurt. She was afraid of her own fragility.

As she contemplated this, she soon understood much about herself that had never been apparent before. She knew nothing of love or caring in the years gone by. As she tried to come to terms with this new emotion that had so changed her, she felt panicked at the vulnerability of self, the uncertainties that beset her. She couldn't handle it, and she couldn't handle seeing Alex.

Then she came to a decision. Looking around for the phone, she managed to grip it awkwardly and pull it off the stand by the bed to sit it on her stomach. She had a hard time dialling the numbers because of her bandaged hand, but she persisted and finally heard the phone on the other end of the connection begin to ring.

'Good afternoon, this is Alex Mason's office, Carrie

speaking—may I help you?' the pleasant female voice on the other end answered.

'Hello, Carrie, this is Diana,' she replied.

'Diana! How are you feeling, dear? I was just planning to come and see you!' Carrie exclaimed with delight at hearing Diana's voice.

'I'm doing really well. The doctor says I have to stay in these casts for too long, though, and then I have to wear a brace on one leg after that!' she sighed in exasperation. 'But I think I'm the lucky one. Alex has it worse than I.'

'You were both lucky,' Carrie said seriously.

After a tiny pause, Diana came right to the point. 'Carrie, I was wondering if you could do something for me. Would you type up a letter if I dictate it to you over the phone and could you bring it when you come to see me tonight?'

'Sure thing,' Carrie affirmed. 'Just let me get a pencil and paper . . . there, I'm all set. Shoot, boss.'

Diana started to dictate and had barely got into the body of the letter when the other woman stopped her.

'This is a letter of resignation! Diana, why?' Carrie interrupted her, aghast.

'I . . . need a vacation,' Diana said lamely. She had been prepared for this kind of reaction but still had not worked out what to say. It really was funny how often lately she had felt like a fool. She, however, didn't laugh as she thought this; it hit too close to home. She'd laugh about it later, later when all the feelings died and peace came back into her life. Then she would sit back and chuckle about how she was head over heels in love with that head guy at—where was it?—Mason Steel, so long ago. Diana did smile at that. Never could she treat it so lightly. There would be no laughs, not from her, not about this.

Carrie was trying to talk her out of the decision when Diana focused back in on the conversation. '. . . please think about it a while longer. There's no need to hurry and you'll have plenty of time to convalesce when you get out of hospital.'

'Carrie, trust me, I know what I want. I—need it for personal reasons. If I put in my resignation now, then I won't have to go back to work out my notice.' Diana now had a note of desperation in her voice. 'Please, Carrie, it's not an impulse. Please!'

Carrie was reluctant to give in. 'I'll finish it if you'll promise me one thing. Will you talk to Alex personally and not just send him a typed letter? Will you do that?'

'I was planning on it,' Diana assured her.

Later that evening, Carrie came to see Diana and gave her the letter to sign, watching her painfully slow efforts to move the pen across the paper. Carrie started to speak, interrupting Diana as she began to say her thanks.

'I talked it over with my husband, Carl, and we both would like to have you come and stay with us for a week or two when you get out of the hospital—now don't say no so quickly!' Carrie forestalled Diana's immediate reaction. 'Please, just think it over. You're going to have a tough time in your apartment all by yourself at first. We think you should stay with someone until you get your casts off at least. Then it should be easier for you to get around. You'd be able to drive yourself to get groceries.'

Diana hesitated. She said finally, 'All right, I'll think about it.'

When she talked to the doctor about Carrie's proposition, he agreed with her. 'You really will need to have someone around to help you at first. Those casts won't be coming off for a while and you're going to be immobile. I'd stay with someone if I were you,' he advised.

'You guys win,' Diana sighed. 'I'll do it.'

After what seemed like a lifetime in the hospital, she was finally able to leave. She tried to look forward to getting out of the uniformly white room that she had been in for so long, but she couldn't manage to feel excitement about anything.

Carrie and Carl helped her to pack and drove her to their comfortable home that was situated well outside the hustle and bustle of New York. They gave Diana her own room on the first floor of the house so that she didn't have to negotiate the stairs and they brought her clothes and personal items from her apartment. She felt ridiculously weak on that first day out of hospital, going straight to bed shortly after arriving. There she lay looking up at the ceiling, tears trickling silently out of the corners of her eyes. Then she fell asleep.

After a few days of living with the Stevens, she began to understand just what a loving household was like. Carrie had two daughters, the older sixteen and the younger fourteen. There was such a lack of tension between the two girls that Diana was amazed. Always before in every home that she had lived in, she had been subject to petty jealousies and comparisons between herself and any of the children in the foster-homes. But in Carrie's home there was nothing but goodnatured ribbing and affection. It was a pleasing atmosphere for Diana, who found herself relaxing more than she ever had in her life.

On a Friday evening, she was lounging on the couch watching the early evening news when Stephanie, the younger one, came bouncing to the couch to throw herself sprawling on one end. She was a thin and gangly-looking girl with braces and a wide, wide smile. Dark blonde hair tumbled anyhow down her back and there was a smattering of freckles across the bridge of her nose. Diana privately thought she was adorable. Stephanie grinned at her, metal winking in the soft light.

'Hiya, hiya, hiya,' she drawled with an atrocious nasal twang. 'Diana, I have a proposition for you.'

'All right, what do you want?' Diana sighed, settling back on her cushions resignedly.

'Want?' Stephanie's eyes rounded as she put on her most innocent of looks. 'My dear, I am the soul of unselfishness, really I am. What could there be that I would want?'

'Obviously you want something.'

'A mere trifle, a slight favour, almost nothing,' Stephanie hummed the words as she stared serenely up at the ceiling.

'You want me to put up your hair again, like I did yesterday?' Diana hazarded a guess.

Stephanie was off of the couch and heading for the hall before Diana could blink. 'I'll get my pins!' came floating over her shoulder as she disappeared.

Seconds later, two somethings hurtled into the living room and turned into human beings as Denise, the older of the two, won the race and deposited herself in front of Diana on the floor. She shrieked 'She promised to put mine up tonight—oh, Stephie—now don't, get off, will you—ow, goldarn it!' The two human girls dissolved into a large something that writhed on the floor as each one tickled the other in order to get the position nearest Diana.

Diana put two fingers in her mouth and whistled piercingly. Instant silence reigned, broken only by Stephanie's exclamation of admiration. 'Golly, Di! Would you teach me that?'

'No way!' Diana told her. 'There's too much noise around here already. Look, I might have a solution to the problem. Who leaves first tonight?'

'I do,' Denise informed her. 'Johnny is picking me up at seven o'clock.'

'I have to be over to Sherrie's house by eight,' Stephanie put in as she plopped into a large chair.

'Easy solution. I'll fix Denise's hair first, then I'll do

yours, Steph,' said Diana. She glanced at her wrist watch. It was twenty minutes to seven. 'That means we've got to hurry, Denise. Are you ready now?'

'Sure thing, jelly bean. Could you fix it in a french braid like last time?' Denise asked, settling herself in easy reach of Diana's hands. 'My hair looked really super—and Johnny iiked it too.'

'Sure thing, jelly bean,' Diana echoed Denise's words. She started to brush Denise's hair with deft fingers. 'Hold still, now! This takes intense concentration.'

Silence and peace settled over the house after the two girls finally left for the evening. Carrie perched in a rocking chair while Diana still laid claim on the couch. They decided to watch a horror movie on the television, and for some minutes, tried to devote all their attention to the screen. But the effort proved to be futile and with a disgusted sigh, Carrie switched off the set and turned to Diana, pulling her chair around as she did so.

'I talked to Alex today,' she told Diana as she relaxed into a rocking pattern. 'I asked him if you'd gotten in touch with him since the accident and he said that aside from a card he received, he hadn't heard from you at all. You promised me you would go and talk with him about resigning.'

'I did.' Diana held up one finger as she talked. 'But I didn't promise when I would talk with him. I want to wait for a while. There's no chance of me going back to Mason Steel, so it really doesn't matter when I talk to him. I just need time.'

Carrie leaned forward in her chair. 'Alex didn't even know where you were staying. He was worried sick about you! Couldn't you at least call him and tell him how you're doing? That wouldn't be so hard, would it?'

'Yes,' she stated baldly. 'Carrie, I didn't resign from Mason Steel because of the work load. I resigned because

I couldn't face Alex day after day.' She stared into Carrie's eyes as she spoke in a low voice. 'Carrie, I just realised in the long hours at the hospital how much I love Alex. I've never loved anyone in my life before. I feel like I've been hit with a sack of bricks! I need time—time to be by myself, because I don't know who I am or what I consider important any more.' She spread out her hands in a gesture of confusion as she shook her head. Carrie listened intently, her face puckered into a concerned frown. She didn't seem surprised by what Diana had just confided.

She said, 'Why don't you tell Alex how you feel? I think you would be surprised by what he would have to say. Please, Diana, you really should air everything out with him.'

Diana shook her head. 'I promised I would see him and talk to him. Let me take things at my own pace. I can't promise anything else right now. Please, Carrie, let's just leave it at that.'

Carrie nodded. She sighed, 'All right, Diana, I won't say anything else.' She was hesitant to ask the question hovering in her mind, but finally did. 'You never talked about the night of the accident and Alex won't speak of it, either. Did something happen at the Paynes' party like you suspected, or did everything go pretty smoothly?'

Diana's face hardened as she heard Alicia's witch-like laughter floating down the hall, again reliving the anguish of that night. 'Oh, everything went smoothly all right,' her lips curled sardonically, as she uttered this. 'Everything was just dandy.' And with that statement, Diana refused to talk about it.

The slow weeks of recovery gradually turned into months as winter began to make its cold and snowy white appearance. As soon as Diana was into a leg brace and out of the casts, she moved into her apartment again, in spite of all the protests that arose in the Stevens household that she stay yet another week.

She spent most of her time lounging in her apartment or taking slow walks in the neighbourhood at the advice of her doctor. She couldn't help but think of Alex and what he must be doing each day. She couldn't help but wonder if he missed her half as much as she missed him. There were no phone calls from him. There were no letters, or any attempts at communication at all. Gradually Diana grew to believe that he didn't even care. She never considered how he would be reading her silence.

Terry and Brenda were worried about her; she could tell by the way they called her almost every day, or how they stopped over with an odd gift of fruit, or a dinner casserole. She was touched by their show of concern, gratefully appreciating every kind and thoughtful gesture, but she stayed silent, wrapped in her own thoughts and daydreams. She was in a cocoon of introspective contemplation. The outside world barely entered into her sphere of thought. She realised in a dreamy sort of way that soon she would have to give some thought to her financial future and what she would like to do with her career, but it hardly made a ripple in the pool of her consciousness. It didn't matter; something would turn up. She was well qualified for a variety of jobs and people with her kind of degree were in demand. She'd take care of it later.

One day she stared at herself in her bedroom mirror and decided suddenly: she would see Alex today, talk with him and try to finally get him out of her life. It was done with no conscious effort, as though she had known all along that it was going to be this day. There was no inward struggle; all of that had gone before. She had no doubt that she would keep loving him for the rest of her life, for it was as impossible to comprehend an end of the emotion as it was for her to comprehend the finality of her own death.

However, Diana didn't have any illusions about the talk. She truly believed that there could be no reconciliation for her love. She knew no other way of existence beside the solitary one she now led. She couldn't allow herself to believe in anything else.

After calling Carrie and confirming a visit for the afternoon, she readied herself and quietly left the apartment.

CHAPTER TEN

A TALL and very slim woman made her way down the sidewalk towards the large steel building that was Mason Steel. She was raven-haired and very striking, drawing looks on that cold and snowy afternoon without even noticing them. It was the unconscious air of dignity and grace that drew attention to her almost painfully thin figure. She limped ever so slightly and yet moved with a fluidity of action that was pleasing to behold. She entered the building swiftly, totally immersed in her own world, uncaring about the outside one.

Diana was stopped several times as she tried to approach the elevator. People from all over the ground floor were pleased to see her, eagerly asking if she was back to work, when she would be back to work, how she was feeling, why she had been away so long. Diana gathered from passing comments that Alex had deliberately kept her resignation a secret as he gambled on whether she would come to talk with him about it or not.

She answered all the questions patiently, considerately spending time with each wellwisher before trying to head to the elevator once more. She was in no hurry; she knew that she would be talking with Alex sooner or later that afternoon. All would come in good time.

In the elevator, Jerry was exuberantly excited to see her, telling her, with a trace of glumness that things 'just ain't been right at all' without her. 'You sure are thin, Miss Carrington,' he grumbled, shaking his head as he eyed her. 'Just like Mr Mason. He's been missing you somethin' awful. Everyday he gets quieter and quieter.

Now he hardly ever says a thing. Boy, he sure looked tired when he first came back to work! Of course, he's lookin' better now, but he still don't look the same, like he used to. He's—harder set in his expressions. He don't laugh as much, neither.'

'I'm sorry to hear that, Jerry,' she said as she watched the light move on the list of floors. She glanced at him. 'But I hardly think that it's because of me; the accident was very severe. Mr Mason nearly didn't make it. He's probably still recovering. I know I am.' Diana was conscious of how true her words really were, more true than Jerry could know. She would be recovering for a long time, a very long time.

Jerry looked sceptical, but refrained from saying anything as the doors opened and Diana left the elevator. He waved goodbye as the doors closed and she waved back, then headed down the hall.

Carrie was in the office rummaging around in the file cabinet when Diana opened the office door. She looked up, then straightened when she saw who it was.

'You've really come,' she stated with satisfaction. 'I was afraid you would change your mind and call me back. I'd told Alex that you promised to come and talk to him some day, but he was beginning to disbelieve me. I'll go and let him know you're here.'

With that, not waiting for a reply, Carrie whisked over to the door and went into the room, shutting the door behind her. Diana stood for a moment in the middle of the floor, then she shrugged off her coat and sat down on the couch. Her heart was pounding. She cursed herself for being a dozen different kinds of fool, but it didn't help her shaking hands or the flush that crept up her face, outlining the edge of her cheekbones.

After a minute or so, Carrie was back informing Diana that Alex would be with her in a moment. He was finishing up a call to California and would send for her when he was free.

Diana's dreamy calm that had been so much a part of her for the last few months deserted her completely and she was seriously considering a mad dash to the door when the other door flew open and Alex stood in front of her. She sat looking at him, not moving or speaking, just staring and taking in every detail of his appearance. He was thinner. There were hollows in his cheeks that hadn't been there before and his facial expression was harder and more sombre, with an air of remoteness that had not been a part of his personality when she had first met him. A small thin scar ran down the side of his face from the temple to the jawline, its rather pinkish newness a silent testimony of the recent crash.

Diana looked at it and started to shake, her mouth trembling as her eyes filled. She shook her head at him in a mute apology for all that had gone before. He had been watching Diana very hard and closely and when he saw the bright gleaming in her eyes, he moved quickly.

'Come on,' he murmured, helping her to stand and walking between her and Carrie as they headed into his office. He closed the door and moved away from Diana, thrusting his hands into the pockets of his slacks and inhaling deeply. Diana limped over to a chair to lean against its support, looking around the room in an effort to regain her composure. It was exactly as she remembered it, down to her desk in the corner of the room. She stared at it.

'Have you found someone to replace me yet?' she asked. The effort at speech steadied her somewhat.

'No. I'm hoping to talk you into coming back.' Alex spoke to the carpet. He was in his usual position against the front of the desk, very still and waiting.

She shook her head at that. 'Oh, no,' she said quietly. It was a very final tone. 'No.'

Alex asked suddenly, 'Are you going to have a limp for the rest of your life?'

She smiled a little. 'I don't know. Sometimes it feels like I am, when I'm especially tired, or my leg is really troubling me. But I don't think I'll have the limp much longer. I really am better—I hardly limp at all if I'm not tired, or if I don't walk too much. Soon you won't be able to tell at all.'

Alex was shaking his head from side to side as Diana told him this. 'You know,' he said when she had finished, 'I wasn't going to mention the accident at all. But when I saw you sitting on the couch, it all seemed to bring everything back so clearly, like a nightmare that one remembers unexpectedly. I wish I'd kept my mouth shut. I'm sorry, Diana.'

'Sorry for what?' she asked gently. 'Sorry for digging all of it up again? I'm not. It—helps to talk to you about it. No one else really understands just what kind of a night that was—the cold, the wet, the fury of the storm. That awful, lasting darkness. I was so afraid you'd been killed. All I could see was a still dark figure that wouldn't answer when I called your name.'

Alex whitened until Diana began to fear that he would pass out. His hands were clenched tightly along the rim of the desk top. 'You mean to say you were conscious that night after the crash?' Diana nodded, looking surprised. She had assumed that Alex knew that. He looked at her, meeting her gaze, and his eyes were sick. 'Oh, my God!' he breathed softly. 'We were there for hours before anyone found us. The one thing I've been telling myself all this time was at least you couldn't know what happened, at least you'd been unconscious, oblivious to any pain. And you were awake the whole time?'

'Oh no,' she hastened to assure him, to ease some of the awful tension in his face. 'I was conscious for a very little while. Most of the time I didn't know what was happening. Really. It wasn't all that bad.'

Alex said softly, 'You're a liar, Diana. But thank you.'

There was a silence, one that each of them found hard to break, one heavy with things unsaid and things needing to be said. Alex stirred. 'May I ask why you won't come back?' he asked with absolutely no expression on his face. Only his eyes were alive, still burning with an intensity that Diana could feel until he once again switched his gaze to the carpet. She tried to speak and had to laugh. It was an unsteady sound.

'I had everything rehearsed, everything,' she said, moving over to the window. The view was dizzying and he looked away. 'I knew what I wanted to say and just now I was going to say it. And then I was going to walk out, leave and never come back. That was my plan "A". I don't have a plan "B", Alex. I just don't know what to say.' She fell silent.

Alex whispered, a curiously intense and desperate sound, 'Try.'

She looked up sharply. 'Yes, I do owe you that.' She took a deep breath, trying to form her thoughts into words. 'Do you remember when we talked a while ago in here, it seems a lifetime ago. I told you that I was looking for something but I didn't know what it was. I didn't know how to look for it, how to achieve it—do you remember it?'

Alex smiled for the first time. 'The bright and shining ideal.'

'Yes, that was it. Oh, Alex, I've been so incredibly stupid! Here I was searching and searching for something that had been right under my nose the whole time. I think it really hit home when I saw you with Alicia that night.' Alex made a sharp sound and would have spoken except

for Diana's interruption. She said quietly, 'Please. I know
I don't deserve it, but just listen to me for a minute.
promise, I'll listen to anything you have to tell me when
I'm done. Please!' Alex stayed silent and Diana said
'Thank you. Always in my life, I would steer clear of
emotional involvement. If you think of my past, you can
understand why. Whenever I felt an attraction for some
one of the opposite sex, I would view it as a threat to
myself. You see, then, when I was struggling to survive, to
make something of myself, I realised that deep down, I
was looking for someone to come and take away all my
problems and to make the world a place of sunshine and
roses. I'd never known love, what it was really like. I just
assumed that this was love, and if this desire that I felt
when I was depressed and discouraged was love, then I
wanted no part of it. It could destroy everything good and
strong that I admired in myself, leaving only self
contempt.

'That's why I didn't recognise what I felt for you until
that night of the car accident. Also, it's why I couldn't
name my emotions until the day in the hospital when they
told me you were going to live. I cried, cried so hard, and
kept thanking God over and over again that you were still
a part of this world. It didn't even matter that you weren't
a part of my world. I just needed to know you were alive.

She moved over to a chair and sat down, absentmindedly rubbing her tired and aching leg. She finished simply,
'In hospital I realised just how much I love you, Alex
I—I think I've loved you ever since you fixed me hot
chocolate and told me to go to bed. No one's ever cared for
me like that before. It just took me so long to understand
how life can be so much more rich, more full. I've
discovered a whole new depth of emotion that I'd never
known could exist, and I thank you and love you for it.

She was looking down at her hands and didn't see him move until he was right beside her.

Alex knelt down on the floor and took her face in between his hands very gently. He searched her eyes with his as he whispered, 'Diana. Oh God, Diana, do you know what you're saying?'

She nodded, her eyes overflowing, wetness splashing his wrists. 'I know,' she whispered back. 'It's taken me all this time to get up the courage to tell you those three simple words. I love you.'

Alex covered her lips with his own as she formed the words without sound. He savoured the feel and the movement, brushing their softness over and over. His actions were like those of a starving man who had just been given a glimpse of a table laden with sustenance. His eyes were closed and his fingers trembled.

Diana reached up an unsteady hand and stroked his thick hair hesitantly. She was shaking violently and she felt weak, defenceless, as if the slightest blow or word would crush her as easily as she might crush an eggshell.

She made an attempt to continue. 'You know, when I saw you with Alicia, I suddenly saw myself in a very different light. She looked so—warm and desirable. I began to see how I would look in about thirty years or so, all thin and shrivelled up, alone and unwanted. I wasn't a very pretty picture to myself. I think that's what I was running from most of all. But I just couldn't escape from myself.'

'Hush!' Alex put a finger against Diana's lips. He caressed them tenderly. 'Hush now, it's my turn to speak. Diana, listen to me very carefully.' He turned her head with lean fingers and made her look at him. 'I was unzipping Alicia's dress because she said the zipper was stuck, that's all. I know it sounds suspicious, it did to me

too, and all I wanted to do was to hurry and get her out o
there. So I helped her with it. She was changing in th
adjoining room. I wasn't expecting her to turn around an
let the dress fall down. That's when you came into th
room.'

He took a deep breath. 'I don't think I'll ever forget th
look on your face as you saw Alicia and me together
Diana, so help me God, I never wanted her that night
How could I? My thoughts were all of you.' He touche
her hair, her face and her neck with such a loving look tha
Diana caught her breath, afraid to believe what he wa
saying.

'You were so beautiful that night,' he murmured,
faraway look in his eyes as he remembered. 'I watched yo
the whole evening, the way you moved and laughed, I'
loved you so much for so long that—'

'What?' she breathed, staring at him, a disbelievin
look in her eyes. 'Love me? You—loved me, love me now?
Alex nodded, picking up her hands and pressing hi
fingers against them.

'And all that time you never guessed!' He had to laugh
little at the expression on Diana's face. 'Oh, my dear,
was so obvious, so glaringly obvious. That was why I wa
so angry with you when you so emphatically put me in m
place that day of the picnic. You are my bright an
shining ideal that I've wanted almost since the day yo
walked into my office for the first time. I was so sure yo
felt an attraction for me too. Then you made such a violen
withdrawal that I was left with my head spinning and
struck back—I think to hurt you as much as you'd hur
me.' Diana shook her head, her eyes agonised as sh
touched him in an effort to dispel the bleak memory in hi
eyes.

Alex looked at her swiftly, the look leaving his face and
light in his eyes beginning to replace it. He bent his hea

suddenly, taking her lips with an unexpectedness that made her draw in her breath quickly. She kissed him back, hungrily pushing her hands under his shirt to touch his pulsing throat and to caress the strong muscles of his chest.

Alex gathered her up into his arms and moved to the largest chair to sit down in it and pull her down on his lap. She snuggled up close to him, her head on his shoulder and her legs curled comfortably around.

He put his mouth on her hair, moving his face in the dark softness and inhaling the fresh scent. A great sigh moved his chest. He spoke softly. 'I want to marry you, Diana. I want to be with you for the rest of my life, to be the one who has the right to touch you and caress you. I want to have you forever.'

'Yes,' she whispered. 'Oh, yes, I want that too.' Alex felt her begin to withdraw a little as she pulled back to look up into his face. 'But, Alex, I'm not ready. No—listen a moment.' She put her hands over Alex's mouth as she shook her head sharply at him. 'I know nothing about love. Nothing. It took me all these months to get to know myself again and I can't handle being rushed. Please, couldn't we take our time and enjoy one another for a while? I need to grow up.'

Alex listened, his face sombre. 'Diana,' he murmured, one hand touching the side of her face. It sounded like a love song. 'I'll wait as long as you want me to, as long as you like. We'll grow together, I promise.'

Later, as they were walking and talking, moving to the parking lot, Alex suddenly asked, 'Are you going to come back to Mason Steel or are you going to look for work somewhere else?'

Diana stopped short. 'Good lord, I never even thought about it! Alex—' she turned towards him, her eyes worried, 'I don't want to come back to Mason Steel. I'm sorry, it's not that I don't—'

'Hush!' Alex put a finger to her lips. He smiled down at her, so big and vital that she wanted to cry out to the world how much she loved him. 'I don't want you to come back unless you want to come back. I want you to do what you want to.' He put his arm around her shoulders as they started to walk again, very slowly.

'But I don't know what I want to do,' Diana protested, her eyes following the cracks in the pavement. 'And I've got to live somehow before we're married.'

'Would you like to start your own business?' Alex suggested. 'You certainly have the ability to.'

'My own business,' Diana echoed. She frowned. 'Where would I get the money for it?'

Alex looked up at the sky, his eyes twinkling with delight. He suggested nonchalantly, 'You could always ask for a loan from your fiancé, you know. I hear he's pretty reasonable about terms.'

Diana looked surprised. She hadn't even thought of him! 'Good heavens—you! Don't look so amused, of course I forgot you had money. And what did you mean about that remark about "terms"? No, forget it! I don't want to know!' Talking and laughing, they made their way to the cars and parted after making plans to meet later that night.

A knock at the door had Diana racing to throw it open, confident as to who it would be. She was right; it was Alex, lean and long as he lazily propped one shoulder against the door jamb and looked down at her with a smile. His hair was tousled and carelessly brushed off his brow and his eyes glowed a fiery blue as they raked down Diana's figure-hugging slacks and woolly sweater. Two deep grooves carved the sides of his mouth as his grin widened.

He had taken in the slight flush on her cheeks that had washed up during his perusal.

'May I come in?' he asked quietly, his voice deep in the silence.

Diana moved jerkily away from the door. 'Of course,' she said, laughing a little unsteadily. 'Have a seat, and I'll go to make some coffee.' She headed for the kitchen, intent on getting out of the room.

'Hey, hey, not so fast!' Alex moved quickly and caught Diana's wrist, pulling her back to him and into the circle of his arms. 'You haven't kissed me yet.' With that, he lowered his head and touched Diana's lips with a light feathery kiss. Diana closed her eyes and moved up her head to deepen the kiss, but Alex moved away, ending it before it had really begun. 'Didn't you say something about coffee?' he asked, laughing down at her face as she looked at him with disappointment.

Diana sniffed, 'It would be more interesting in the kitchen, anyway.' She squealed as Alex slapped her sharply on the behind. 'I'm going, all right!' She disappeared.

She put the coffee automatically in the machine as she thought of Alex in the next room. 'Make yourself comfortable,' she called out, finishing the coffee-making procedure with efficient movements. She poked her head out of the kitchen doorway and saw Alex seated in a big chair in the living room. 'Did you want something to eat?' she asked.

He shook his head. 'Not really, unless you did.' She shook her head too and disappeared again.

Carrying the loaded tray into the living room, she set it down on the small table by the sofa and saw the box. She stopped.

Alex, watching her reactions, said quietly, 'I went shopping for it after we talked. I wanted to surprise you with something special. If you don't like it, we can take it back and pick something out together.'

Diana shook her head, still staring at the small black box without touching it. She jumped when Alex touched her arm. He motioned for her to pick it up and she did slowly, almost as if she were afraid the box would bite her. She opened the lid and gasped. Flashes of light seemed to come from within the little box and she turned it back and forth to make the ring catch the light. There was a large diamond in the centre of the ring, with two smaller diamonds in a swirling design on either side of the centre. It was a slim and elegant ring, made for slim and elegant hands.

Alex took the box and the ring, then pulled the ring from its resting place and slid it on Diana's ring finger on her left hand. She stared fascinated at the winking bright diamond in the centre of the ring. It was a perfect fit.

After a moment, Alex asked, 'Do you like it?' She turned to him, her eyes shining.

'Do I like it?' she repeated. 'Of course I like it—no, I take that back. I love it!' She moved over to him and put her arms around him, kissing him unrestrainedly. She whispered, 'It's perfect, you couldn't have picked a more beautiful ring.'

Alex slid his arms around her and pulled back his head to look into her eyes. 'I'm glad,' he said simply. 'I wanted you to like it.'

Diana nodded, speaking thoughtfully, 'Only now we have to think of a date for the wedding.'

'A wedding date!' he exclaimed. 'I thought you wanted a little time to yourself before we rushed into marriage?'

'I do, I do,' she assured him. 'But I was thinking in a matter of five or six months or so, and that's not a lot of time to plan a wedding.'

Alex threw back his head and laughed. 'And I thought

you meant to wait a year or two and I was wondering how I was going to stand waiting that long! Oh, Diana, I love you!' And with that, he took her lips while still chuckling. She started to smile under his lips and he opened one eye to stare at her, then straightened quickly. He muttered, 'Why do I feel like I've lost my audience?' But she wasn't paying attention.

'Alex, we really should send Alicia a wedding announcement, don't you think?' She chuckled as she said it.

Alex started to grin. 'Poetic justice? I'd like to see her face as she opened it up to read it. Now, that would be a picture!' He turned serious and pulled Diana closer in his arms, murmuring softly, 'But why are we talking about her when we have better things to think about?' He bent his head and they didn't talk again for a very long time.

CHICKEN DIVAN

Despite the demands of her career, Diana, Amanda Carpenter's hardworking heroine, still finds the time to cook. On one occasion she makes herself a broccoli casserole; on another, she shares a chicken casserole with friends. No doubt, then, that Diana would have enjoyed the following casserole that combines chicken and broccoli —a tempting dish called Chicken Divan.

What you need:

2 whole chicken breasts, halved and deboned	1½ cups chicken broth
1 tbsp. vegetable oil	¼ cup dry white wine
8-10 broccoli spears	¼ cup sour cream
2 tbsp. butter	⅓ cup sharp cheddar cheese, grated
3 tbsp. flour	

What to do:

In hot skillet, brown chicken in oil. Turn heat to medium and cook, turning occasionally, a further 20 minutes. Meanwhile steam broccoli till just lightly cooked (3-4 minutes). Grease a casserole dish and place broccoli on bottom. In a saucepan, melt butter. Remove from heat, blend in flour. Add broth, combine well and return to heat. Stirring constantly, cook until sauce bubbles. Add wine, remove from heat and fold in sour cream. Pour half of sauce over broccoli. Place chicken on top, then cover with remaining sauce. Sprinkle with cheddar and bake, uncovered, in a 350°F. (175°C.) oven for 20 minutes. Serves 4.